What
Happened
to Normal?

What Happened to Normal?

A Novel

LORI SCHUR

What Happened to Normal?

Published through Lori Schur

ISBN: 979-8-218-68572-0 (Paperback Edition)
ISBN: 979-8-218-68571-3 (eBook Edition)

For my son Justin
You are my reason.
I love you!
Mom

The Early Years

One

I'm sitting on the floor in what I will always refer to as my son's playroom surrounded by large blue bags, piles of clothes, bedding, and towels. Beside me is a pad and pen with a list pages long of everything Sean will need as he moves away. I tuck my hair behind my ears as I lean back against the wall, feeling a little overwhelmed thinking about how much time was spent in this room over the past eighteen years. Each corner of this room tells a story. The spot where he took his first steps. The wall where we hung his basketball hoop, which he played with every single day. The couch where he sat to read books. In my mind's eye I can see the puzzles, toys, games, the Buzz Lightyear figure and a very loved, worn-out Elmo so clearly spread out over the carpet that is now covered with all the essentials every college freshman needs. WOW! How did we get here?

My thoughts are interrupted by the clanging sound of the garage door opening. Jumping to my feet, I head down the hallway just as Sean drops his bookbag on the kitchen floor.

"Hi honey! How was your day?" I call out as I round the corner and enter the room.

"It was great! I'm starving," he says, as he rummages through the pantry looking for snacks. "Mrs. Hannigan gave us our schedules for our senior project presentations. I'm next Wednesday morning at ten."

I reach to grab a pen and write the information on the oversized calendar sitting on the counter, then, looking ahead, I realize there are only three more weeks until we enter senior graduation week. Five full days of activities for the seniors, faculty and parents leading up to the grand finale, graduation day. I get teary-eyed just thinking about it. I'm such a mixed bag of emotions. I'm elated for Sean, full of pride to be a part of his school and their traditions and at the same time, I can't help but feel a touch of sadness, as I'm hyperaware that time is moving way too fast.

As he finishes off a quickly made sandwich, Sean smiles at me. "Mom, I'm running over to Noah's house. What time is dinner?"

"Six o'clock. Same as every night. Have fun, but don't be late."

I abandon the project in the playroom to start prepping dinner and not five minutes after Sean leaves the house, David walks through the door, calling my name.

"I'm in the kitchen!" I yell over my shoulder.

After a quick kiss, he starts rummaging through

the fridge. "Jessie, what's for dinner? I'm starving." Like father, like son.

"Meatloaf and baked potatoes. How was your day?"

"It was good. I pitched a marketing campaign strategy to a new client today and I think it went well. Where's Sean?"

"He ran over to Noah's for a little bit before dinner."

"Ok, I'm going to change and go relax," David says as he leaves the kitchen.

After I prep dinner, I make a cup of tea and carry it with me out onto the sundeck. It's a beautiful day and as I look out over the yard, I can't help but think about what the next few months are going to be like. Graduation, then a quick summer trip to the beach, a trip north to visit family and finally, new student orientation and move-in day. Is this really happening? Sitting down in my favorite rocking chair, I take a deep breath and slowly exhale.

Just as I begin to relax, my phone dings. It's a text from Sean. "Mom, don't forget to look for pictures I can submit for the senior assembly. They're suggesting a minimum of five photos that I have to turn in tomorrow."

Of course you do, I think. I send him a thumbs-up and take my cup of tea with me as I walk back to the playroom. In the closet are all my photo albums and scrapbooks that tell the story of us. I pull them out and sift through the albums, trying to decide which pictures to hand over to Sean, and as I turn the pages, my mind is flooded with memories.

One picture, in particular, causes me to catch my breath. It was the summer of 2009. Sean was eight years old. We were sitting at the hotel pool on Hilton Head Island and Sean had just gotten out of the water and was wrapped in a big, fluffy, sky-blue towel. His face, bearing a huge smile as if he were mid-laugh, was tilted toward the sun. My fingers trace the outline of his face and smile. I remember sitting on the edge of the lounge chair as I captured that picture. *Oh, my sweet boy. We were both so innocent, with no idea what was to come,* I think to myself. It was the last picture I took before our lives were forever changed.

Two

At the end of May, 2009, third grade is officially complete! My eight-year-old is on summer break and I couldn't be happier. Summer in the Carolinas is hot, humid and long, but I love it! In just a few weeks we'll have our toes in the sand at our favorite beach on Hilton Head Island, enjoying our annual summer vacation. We are shopping for last minute items for our trip when Sean grabs his stomach and says he has pain and needs to use the bathroom. We rush to the back of the store to find the restrooms and I wait for what feels like a very long time for him to come out, when he finally does and says, "Mom, can we go home?" When I ask him what's wrong, he says, "I feel better but I'm tired and want to go home." We quickly check out and as soon as we get home, he goes into his playroom and I head into the kitchen. When I check on him, he is sitting on the floor playing with a game. "How are you feeling, honey?"

"My stomach still hurts." He moves his hand around his bellybutton area. I'm not an alarmist, but I have this weird mom vibe telling me that something's not right. When I talk to my sister as I'm relaying the incident, I feel a sense of urgency. "Kim, I'm going to hang up and call the doctor."

Short Falls Pediatrics encourages me to come right over. When we get there, our favorite nurse, Judy, calls us back. She checks his height, weight and temperature and Sean tries to describe the stomach pains he is experiencing. Judy tells me Dr. Matheson will be in shortly. Short Falls has eight pediatricians on staff so you never know in advance who you will see at a sick visit. Dr. Matheson is new to the practice, so we haven't met him in person, although I remember seeing his picture and bio when they introduced him in their monthly newsletter. We're playing "I spy" when Dr. Matheson walks in. He is young, around five-foot-seven, with a slight build, round, John Lennon-type glasses, and a very guarded smile.

"Hey, buddy, what's up? I hear your stomach hurts," he says to Sean, as he nods and extends his hand to me. "I'm Dr. Matheson." I shake his hand and look over to Sean. "Can you tell Dr. Matheson where your stomach hurts?"

Sean shows him where the pain is. The doctor has him lie on the exam table and feels around his stomach, listens to his lungs, looks at me very confidently and says, "I think it's gas. Try giving him over-the-counter gas medicine before his meals. He should be fine." Simple enough.

A few days later, Sean is again complaining of stomach pains, but now, in addition to the stomach pain, he seems a little moody from time to time, which is unsettling, because when I tell you this boy is so chill, I'm not exaggerating. Again, I take him to the doctor and again we see Dr. Matheson. He feels around Sean's stomach and says it's nothing to worry about. "Just gas," he says. Again. Ok. I will give it some time. I feel a little dismissed, but with no other symptoms to point to, we leave the office and continue with the gas relief tablets. Feeling hyper-sensitive to any little symptom, I notice at dinner Sean's appetite is not as hearty as usual and start keeping a journal of my observations.

A week later and two days before our beach trip to Hilton Head, Sean is again complaining about his stomach and saying he doesn't feel well. He also says his eyes are a little blurry. For the third time in less than a month, I'm back at the pediatrician's office. Once again, we have the good fortune of seeing Dr. Matheson. A practice with eight doctors who rotate offices and shifts, and we keep getting assigned to the same doctor! I'm starting to feel uneasy with him and losing confidence in his assessment. I'm also sensing he thinks I'm an over-anxious mom who keeps coming back for no reason, and he is humoring me by examining Sean, which consists of just feeling around his stomach. When I mention that he complained of blurry eyesight, he sighs and has him read the eye chart on the back of the door. Sean aces it and once again, we are sent home with no diagnosis.

We leave two days later for Hilton Head, which turns out to be relaxing and peaceful. We build sandcastles on the beach and swim in the hotel pool, play many rounds of mini-golf, and enjoy scenic walking trails. I'm watching Sean like a hawk and, while there is nothing specific I can point to, he just seems off. For a child who is usually so full of energy, constantly in motion, always wanting to throw a ball or run around, he seems sluggish and lethargic. I'm also suspicious about his dwindling appetite. When we are having dinner at his favorite pizza place and waiting for our food, Sean keeps telling us how he is starving, but when our food finally arrives, he eats one piece of pizza and says he is full, which is extremely unusual for him. I add this to my journal and make a mental note to schedule a physical as soon as we get home. On our final day, Sean is worn out from swimming and is content to sit wrapped in his fluffy blue towel on a lounge chair by the pool. I'm holding my camera and as I lean over, Sean lifts his chin to the sun, and with the towel framing his face, he smiles the brightest smile I've ever seen, causing me to smile back as I capture the picture.

Three

Monday morning comes a little too quickly and brings with it a return to our normal lives. It's Sean's first day at Happy Trails Camp, where his days will be full of sports, arts and crafts, swimming, game time and tons of activities. His best friends, Cory and Billy, go to the same camp, and since they go to different schools during the year, they look forward to hanging out every day together. David is back to work, where he leads the creative team for a national marketing firm, and while his days are hectic, he is flexible with his schedule and tries to come home early in the summer. I work part-time three days a week as an administrative assistant for a professional recruiting and staffing firm and spend my days off volunteering at our synagogue, where I am president of our sisterhood group. As president, I oversee a group of ladies who plan family activities and fellowship opportunities for the women of the congregation. We just hired a new rabbi, and so our most pressing event is organizing her welcome service and reception.

I drop Sean off at camp, and barely get a good-bye as he is so eager to get inside and see his friends, and then drive to work. Walking into the office, I am greeted by my boss, Ellen, sitting at the front desk. She hangs up the phone, looks up at me and pretends to be exasperated. "Thank heaven you're back!" She hands me a stack of resumés and says, "These have to be entered into the system and once that's done, you'll need to contact the applicants to set up appointments for preliminary interviews."

"Good to see you, too!" I laugh as I head toward my desk.

"I hope you had a good rest, because it's been non-stop since you left." Ellen waves over her shoulder as she walks into her office. I grab a cup of coffee and get to work. Five hours later, every prospect has been entered and contacted, and I gather my things to leave. I go straight home to work on the rabbi's reception. With less than two weeks left to pull it all together, I am feeling a little overwhelmed, and the afternoon flies by as I focus on all the details. Before I know it, I am back in the car picking up Sean from camp. He jumps in the car with more energy than I've witnessed lately, and just as I'm about to pull away, Melanie waves her hands to stop me, sticks her head in the window and says, "Hey Jess...I only have a minute, but I wanted to give you a heads-up. Sean seemed exceptionally thirsty today and had to run inside several times to use the restroom. Unusual for him, but then again, it's so hot that he may just be drinking more from the heat. Just thought I should mention it to you."

"Thanks, Melanie. I'll keep an eye on him. See you tomorrow." I wave as I pull away from the camp, then I steal a look at Sean through the rear-view mirror and ask, "How was your day?" as I navigate the car out of the parking lot.

"Great. Cory got to go to New York to a Yankees game last week and he got a baseball signed by Derek Jeter! How cool is that?"

"Very cool. How is Billy? Did he have fun last week too?" I'm friends with both their moms but I haven't had a chance to catch up with them since we got back from the beach.

"He did. They went to Florida to visit his grandma. I'm starving...did you bring a snack?"

I reach into my bag and toss him a Rice Krispie treat. "Sweet," he says as he rips open the package and starts to eat.

Once we get home, Sean runs to his playroom to power up his gaming console and I pick up the phone to make an appointment for his physical. Linda, the receptionist, tells me that the first available appointment is three weeks away, which I say is fine, as long as it's not with Dr. Matheson. I write the date on my calendar and head straight to the kitchen to start making dinner. I'm pulling the chicken out of the fridge when I hear the garage door open. David comes through the door carrying a box.

"I bought Sean a new putter. Thought I'd take him

out to play nine holes of golf on Saturday." He kisses my cheek as he places the box on the counter.

"That sounds like fun! Make your tee time later in the day and I'll meet you after for dinner."

David gives me a thumbs-up as he walks toward our bedroom to change out of his work clothes. I turn my attention back to the kitchen where I prep dinner and put it in the oven. Tonight's specialty is baked chicken with pasta and a vegetable. Ok, let's be real for just a minute... baked chicken is my "go-to" dinner several days during the week. What changes is the side dish. I do occasionally make a meatloaf or meatballs, but I'm a creature of habit and David and Sean are picky eaters. Besides, I'm not the best cook. I tell David all the time that when I win the lottery the first thing I'm doing is hiring a chef. Of course, you have to play the lottery to win the lottery, so that may not be happening any time in the near future! A girl can dream though.

Four

Friday after work, I attend a meeting at the synagogue with some of the congregants who are participating in the service. Everyone is excited because we've hired a musician to accompany the rabbi as she sings some of the prayers for this special service, and have scheduled a rehearsal for next Monday afternoon, plenty of time before Friday's service. My phone alarm rings, reminding me it's time to pick Sean up from camp. After packing up my things, I wish the rabbi a good shabbat and make my way to the car. Pulling into the camp parking lot a little later than usual, I'm stuck at the back of the pickup line, so I put the car in park, close my eyes and rest for a few minutes until the car behind me honks their horn. I give a little wave in my rearview mirror and pull up to the front, where Melanie, the camp director, is standing with Sean. As he gets into the car, Melanie tells me that Sean had to rest a few times today because he seemed to get overheated. She gave him some juice and a snack, and he bounced back, but wanted to be sure to let me know.

"Hey, Buddy," I say as I look at Sean through the rearview mirror. "How was your day? Are you feeling ok?"

"Yup...I feel fine. I had a great day. We got to play dodge-ball inside this afternoon. Our counselor said it was too hot to play outside. My team won!" Then he leans his head back on the seat as he gazes out the window. I make a mental note to call the pediatrician's office first thing Monday morning to ask if we can move up the date for Sean's physical.

We have a fun weekend and Sunday night I should have been exhausted, but as soon as we get into bed and turn out the lights David is gently snoring, and I toss and turn for an hour before deciding that lying there is fruit-less. I tiptoe down the hall to the family room, grab a magazine and a blanket, and curl up on the couch. A few articles in, I come across an interview with Nick Jonas's mom. She is sharing her experience when Nick was diagnosed with type 1 diabetes. As I read her story, I start getting a chill down my spine. Something in the way she describes how almost overnight Nick lost a lot of weight and then describes her guilt at not recognizing it sooner makes me catch my breath. I start sweating and feel a rise of panic. *What if I'm missing something? What if there is something seri-ously wrong and the doctors keep brushing it off?* I tell myself there is no way Sean can have type 1 diabetes. I remind myself that for the most part he is feeling good and playing sports and, other than his decrease in appetite, he seems ok. Still, I can't settle my nerves. I put the magazine away and make my way back to bed, promising myself I am call-ing Short Falls Pediatrics first thing in the morning.

After a very restless night's sleep, I'm hustling to drop Sean off at camp the next morning and get to work when the rabbi calls to confirm our rehearsal that afternoon. I pull into the office parking lot at the same time as Ellen, so I quickly hang up with the rabbi, and we walk in together while she gives me a rundown of our day. I'm so immersed in my work that it takes me a minute to realize my phone is vibrating. I look down to see it's eleven-thirty a.m. and Melanie is calling.

The minute I say "hello" Melanie wastes no time. "Jess, I think you need to come get Sean. I'm sure it's just a little dehydration but he's not feeling well. He was outside playing soccer and started to feel dizzy. He's trying to cool off, but he looks very flushed and he's drinking a ton of water."

As she is talking, I grab my purse, rush into Ellen's office, pointing to the phone, and mouth "Gotta go." Then I run out the door, cutting Melanie off to say, "I'm on my way." At the next light I call the pediatrician's office.

"Linda, it's Jessie Greene. Something is wrong with Sean. I'm picking him up from camp and bringing him straight to your office. Is Dr. Sharon in today?"

"Hi Mrs. Greene. Yes, Dr. Sharon is here. I'll put you on her schedule."

"Thanks, Linda. It may take me about thirty minutes but I'm on my way. Do not let her leave for lunch. I'm really worried."

Accelerating through every yellow light, I make exceptional time getting to the camp. Sean looks tired and now that I'm looking at him, he looks thin. He gets into the car, and we hightail it over to Short Falls Pediatrics. On our way, Sean says he's starving so I reach into my bag, hand him a snack and by the time we get to the office he seems a little more like himself. Linda checks us in, and the nurse immediately calls us back. As she notes Sean's weight, I am shocked to discover he has lost seven pounds since our last visit. It's only been two weeks. As soon as we get into the room, Dr. Sharon walks in, and I'm so relieved to see her. She has cared for Sean since he was born. She's also a mom with kids of her own. She gets it. She reviews the notes in his chart, asking us questions about Sean's stomach issues, focusing on the frequent trips to the bathroom, his loss of appetite and how tired he appears at times. The wave of panic is rising within me as I answer all her questions.

She looks at me calmly and says, "I'm going to check his blood and urine and let's see if we can figure out what's going on." Then she looks at Sean and asks, "Are you up for peeing in a cup?" Seriously, an eight-year-old boy? Challenge accepted. She gives us a cup and we head to the bathroom. Once I'm sure he knows what to do I step out to give him some privacy. He puts the cup in the little box in the wall and washes up, then walks out grinning.

"That was fun." He laughs as we head back to the examining room.

As soon as we walk in, Nurse Judy is waiting for us. She takes a little needle, sticks the side of his finger and fills a few slides with his blood. Then she takes a hand-held machine, places a thin, flat test strip in it and draws blood onto the strip. A number lights up on the machine, but I can't make it out from where I'm sitting. Watching her as she records the number, I see a wave of concern pass over her face, but just as quickly her smile returns, and she gives Sean a pat on the shoulder and says, "Dr. Sharon will be right in." Then she leaves the room before I can ask any questions.

I call David and start filling him in when Dr Sharon walks back in, and she doesn't look like her cheerful self. She rubs Sean's back as she looks at me and shakes her head. Before she can say a word, I let her know David is on the phone and put it on speaker so he can hear what she has to say.

Still rubbing Sean's back, she looks me in the eye and very calmly says "Jessie, I'm concerned that Sean may have type 1 diabetes. His blood sugar is very high, and he has ketones in his urine." She pauses and I stare at her thinking, *what the heck are ketones?* Before I can ask, she continues, "You need to take Sean directly to the ER at Children's Hospital. They will be expecting you, so no stopping in between. Go straight there. They will take good care of you."

Five

At the hospital I search the waiting room for David but he's not there yet. As soon as we've checked in at reception though, I spot him walking through the doors. Sean runs to him and wraps his arms around David's waist. Still holding him tight, David leans in and hugs me with his other arm. In his eyes I see the same fear and panic I feel, but outwardly, we both smile at Sean and take a seat. The minute we sit down, they call our names, and we are up and moving through a second set of doors. With each step I start talking to myself. *We are going to be ok. This is a big mistake. His blood sugar was high from the snack in the car. I'm sure he's fine now. We are going to laugh about this later.*

They take us into an empty patient room up on the ninth floor and a nurse quickly enters and introduces herself as Mary. She tells us to make ourselves comfortable and a doctor will be in shortly to talk to us. Sean sits on the bed and turns on the TV, changing the channel to ESPN. There's a golf tournament on and Sean and David are captivated, talking about the golfers and the course. Sports is a big part of our life — in our house it's all sports all the time, bouncing between football, basketball, hockey, and golf. So with David and Sean distracted by the tournament, I sit down in the chair, look out the window, take a deep breath and try to process what is happening. But I'm cut short when two men wearing white coats with stethoscopes around their necks walk into the room. One is tall, blond, wears glasses and has a kind, welcoming face. The shorter one is dark-haired, a little more guarded and serious-looking.

The taller one with the glasses introduces himself as Dr. Neely. David and I introduce ourselves as we shake hands. He then motions to the short, brooding one and says, "This is my colleague, Dr. Sharpe." Dr. Sharpe nods and shakes hands with us, as Dr. Neely crouches down so he is eye level with Sean. After they high five he tells Sean that they are going to run a few tests and then he will be back to talk to us. Sean tells him he is hungry and the doctor reminds him he needs to wait to eat until we finish all the tests. "Just a little while longer," he says as he stands up. He smiles at us in an "I'm-sorry-this-is-happening" kind of way and tells us the nurse will be in to draw some blood and they will be back as soon as they can with the results.

I'm so nervous now. It's one thing to stick his finger. It's another whole level of worry when they wheel in a cart with multicolored tubes and those rubber bands they tie around your arm to get your veins to pop. Sean has always had a fear of needles. I'm not talking about the *I-don't-want-a-shot* fear. I'm talking about the *hiding-under-the-exam-table, begging-them-not-to-come-near-him-with-that-needle* fear. How are we ever going to deal with this?

Six

A young woman walks into our room and introduces herself as Madison. She is bright, cheerful and smiles at Sean as she sits down. She tells us she is a child life specialist, and her job is to make sure Sean is comfortable and calm, and to help him through the stress of his hospital experience. She starts talking to him as the nurse comes in to draw his blood, and I watch in awe as they explain every detail of what they are about to do. Madison gently takes Sean's hand and continues to talk to him as the nurse works on his other arm and begins to draw the blood. She fills so many vials I lose count. Before I know it, the nurse is leaving the room and Sean and Madison are laughing at some story Madison told him. David and I look at each other with relief. Shortly after the nurse leaves, Madison gets up and says her goodbyes, with promises to stop back again later in the afternoon. It's now two p.m. and I realize I never gave Ellen an explanation for leaving, never called the rabbi to tell her I wouldn't be at rehearsal and have missed several calls from Melanie. Leaving David and Sean, who are back to watching ESPN, I step outside to call them.

I call the rabbi first, leaving a brief voicemail letting her know we had a health issue to deal with, reassure her I feel confident that all the details are handled for Friday night and will be in touch later in the week. Next, I leave a message for Ellen promising to call her when I have more information. Finally, I call Melanie who picks up right away. I tell her what's happened since we left camp.

"Oh, Jessie...I'm so sorry. But I know everything will be ok. Sean is going to be fine. Whatever it is, I'm here for you." I start to choke up. "Thanks, Melanie. I have to go, but I will let you know when we hear the results."

We hang up and, leaning against the wall with my eyes closed, I start pleading with God. *Please don't let it be diabetes. Please, please, let my baby be ok.*

David gives me a weak smile as I walk back into the room and sit down in the one and only chair by the window. He is lying on the bed with Sean cuddled up next to him when the nurse comes in to check on us briefly and, using the same machine Dr. Sharon's office used, draws some blood onto a test strip. She shields the number so I can't see, but I can tell from the look on her face it's not good. She assures us it won't be much longer and then gently places her hand on my arm. "As soon as they get the lab results the doctor will be back to talk with you."

I close my eyes and return to my "pleading-with-God" conversation. There's still time before they come in this room with results. *Please let it be ok.*

David clears his throat, and I glance over toward the bed. He nods toward Sean, who is now asleep, while he slowly pulls away and untangles himself from the blanket. Motioning for me to follow him, we step out into the hallway, where he pulls me close and whispers in my ear.

"He is going to be ok. No matter what they tell us, we are all going to be ok."

I hug him tighter and just nod my head. We lean against the wall and talk in whispers about nothing in particular. I think we both want to know we can be "normal" when none of this feels normal. The waiting is excruciating. I finally cave and look up at David.

"I wish they would just tell us what's going on. We've been here for hours, and no one is giving us any answers."

"Be patient," he whispers, as he hugs me a little tighter.

"Mom?" Sean is standing in the doorway watching us.

"Hey, buddy. Did you have a good nap?"

"Yeah. But I'm hungry and I want to go home."

Me too bud...me too, I think, as I lead him back into the room. It's now four-thirty p.m. and Sean hasn't eaten since that snack in the car on the way to Dr. Sharon's office. I glance over at the chair where I left my phone. It's buzzing and when I look to see who's calling, I realize I've missed ten calls. Two from the rabbi, two from Melanie and the rest from Sherry and Karen. Sherry is Billy's mom, and Karen is Cory's mom, and we all spend a lot of time together with our "three musketeers," as we call them. By now they would have picked the boys up from camp and I'm sure they got an earful about how Sean had to leave early because he wasn't feeling well. I so badly wish we were waving from the car line instead of sitting in this hospital room waiting to learn my child's fate. I toss the phone into my purse, so I don't have to see it light up, frustrated that I have no answers and no bandwidth to call anyone right now.

Seven

Having made an executive decision to change the channel in an attempt to find something we can mindlessly watch, I'm flipping through the menu on the screen when Dr. Neely and Dr. Sharpe walk in. Dr. Neely sits on the end of Sean's bed as Dr. Grumpy, aka Dr. Sharpe, stands to his side. I watch them and wonder which one is going to revive me because I feel like I might pass out. David comes around and puts his hand on my shoulder.

"I'm hungry," Sean announces, breaking the ice.

Dr. Neely smiles at him and says, "How about we have a little chat and then you can go get something to eat?" Then he looks at me and David and says, "Does anyone in your family have type 1 diabetes?" When we both shake our heads no, he continues.

"Type 1 diabetes is an autoimmune disease. Basically, the body's immune system attacks and destroys insulin-producing cells in the pancreas, causing your pancreas to stop making insulin. Your body needs insulin to move the sugar from your bloodstream into your muscles. If your body is not producing insulin, the sugar stays in your bloodstream, causing you to have high blood sugars." He pauses to look at Sean, then at us. Sean is staring at him with a blank look on his face. I think this is way over his head. We are in shock, trying to absorb what he is saying. He just nods and continues.

"A normal blood sugar reading should fall between seventy and 125. When Sean was admitted his blood sugar was 450. After running many tests, we are sorry to tell you that Sean has type 1 diabetes." Again, he pauses, looks around the room and continues.

"We spoke to the Pediatric Endocrinology office. They have reviewed all his results and agree with this diagnosis. We are admitting Sean for the night and will start him on insulin right away. Tomorrow morning you'll go to the Peds Endo office, where they will teach you how to give Sean insulin shots and care for him." Again, he pauses. Again, we all stare at him.

As he continues to talk and explain the intricacies of type 1 diabetes, I feel myself slowly losing focus. I see his mouth moving, but his voice sounds like it's muffled and, as much as I try to concentrate, all I can hear is diabetes, insulin shots, no cure. I look down and notice my hands are trembling. *Focus, Jessie. You need to understand everything he says.* I look up and will myself to pay attention.

"Mr and Mrs. Greene, Sean is going to be ok. It will be an adjustment, but he will be just fine. The nurse will be in to give him his first shot and then you can take him downstairs to the cafeteria to eat dinner." Dr. Neely gets up and pats Sean on the shoulder as he turns to leave. Before he makes it to the door, I speak up.

"How can we fix this?"

His response frightens me. "You can't fix this. You can only treat this."

David follows them out into the hallway. I hear them whispering as I turn to Sean. I sit down and take him into my arms.

"Do you have any questions?" I ask him. He shakes his head and rests it against my shoulder.

"I just want to go home," he whispers.

Eight

The nurse comes in holding a hand-held device with a test strip, a vial of insulin and a syringe. She smiles at Sean and leans down, so she is eye level with him. "Hi Sean, I'm going to take a little blood from your finger first. Can I have your hand?" Sean holds out his hand and she gently takes it, running an alcohol swab over the side of his finger and then quickly sticks that same spot to draw some blood. She holds the test strip up to the blood and a number appears on the device – 345. *Well, that's not good*, I'm thinking, as she stands up and makes some notes in her computer. She then draws some insulin into the syringe, swabs his arm and says "Quick and easy. Just look at mom." Sean looks my way as she quickly injects his arm and it's over before he realizes it. WOW. I am in awe at how she handled that and more impressed with Sean. My little boy with the needle phobia seems to intuitively understand that we have no options here.

Fighting back tears and trying to keep my voice from shaking, I smile at my son. "Sean, you are so brave. We are so proud of you." The nurse smiles at us both and says, "Enjoy your dinner. I'll see you later."

David and I usher Sean toward the door and down the hallway to the elevator. I try to keep my eyes focused in front of me and not glance in the other rooms. So many children here. So many parents hurting for them. This feels so surreal. I keep thinking I'm going to wake up in my bed at home with Sean down the hall and this will be nothing but a bad dream, and I hold onto that fantasy, which bursts as soon as the elevator chimes and the doors open. We step inside and make our way down to the first floor. Sean is so hungry he is starting to lose his patience. We step out of the elevator, and he starts to cry, claiming he is so hungry he can't take another step. I wrap my arm around him, point to the end of the hall and say, "Dinner is waiting right around that corner. You can do this! I'll race you there!" He perks up and starts to run.

"He never does back down from a challenge," David observes, laughing as he catches up to us.

While Sean and I get a table, David orders our food. He brings back a tray full of burgers and fries and before I can pass the ketchup Sean is digging in. The table is silent; we're all trying to digest what has happened over the last few hours. David and I agree that I will go home and pack a few things so I can spend the night with Sean, and since we have to leave the hospital early in the morning to go to the Pediatric Endocrinologist office, David will go home to get some sleep and meet us there in the morning.

After dinner, I walk them to the elevator for their trip back upstairs. Sean has a few requests of items to bring from home, which I assure him I will, and a tear slips from my eye as I hug David. Quickly, I wipe it away and smile at them as they get in the elevator, but once the doors close, I lose control and the tears fall. *How did this happen? How did we end up here? How am I going to take care of my little boy?* The tears continue to fall all the way to the car, where I sit for a minute, feeling so scared. But eventually, taking deep breaths, I wipe my eyes and head home.

On my way there, I call my sister Kim. She answers on the second ring and the minute I hear her voice I start to cry again. Barely able to catch my breath, I tell her what's happening, asking her to please call our parents and brother because I don't think I have the strength to explain it again. "Just let them know we are ok and will call as soon as we can." She offers words of encouragement, which only make me cry harder. Promising to call her tomorrow, I hang up so I can concentrate on driving.

The minute I walk into the house, my phone rings. I don't want to talk to anyone, but I'm worried it might be David or the hospital calling, so I answer.

"Jessie, it's Mom." *Like I don't recognize her voice,* I think, as I sigh and brace myself.

"Hi Mom. Are you ok?" I ask.

"Am I ok? Are you ok?" That's all it takes to make me cry again.

"Jessie, I can get a flight out first thing in the morning. Do you want me to come?"

"Mom, I love you for that, but no, I don't. We have so much to learn, and we need a little time to adjust. I'd rather you come when we're settled and can enjoy your visit."

"Ok, but if you change your mind, I'm on the next flight. Give Sean hugs and kisses and call me when you all get home tomorrow. I love you, Jessie."

"I love you too, Mom. I will call when I can."

Tears are streaming down my face as I pull together a few things to get us through the night. After throwing some snacks in my bag, it dawns on me that I have no idea what he is allowed to eat. The sorrow is overwhelming me as I close my overnight bag, grab my keys and head back to the hospital.

Nine

When I walk into his room, Sean is playing a video game connected to his TV and David is sitting in the chair by the window, staring straight ahead. Faking a smile, I lean down to kiss Sean on the forehead and take David's hand.

"Where did the video game come from?" I ask David.

"Madison brought in a cart full of games and movies and Sean got to choose whatever he wanted." Sending Madison a silent thank-you, I give David's arm a little pull.

"How about you go home and rest? It's been a long day."

"Are you going to be able to sleep here in this chair?"

"I'll be fine. Go home, honey."

He stands up, gives Sean a kiss on the cheek, and says, "I'll see you in the morning, Sean." Sean smiles up at him, then goes right back to his game while we walk out of the room.

We hold onto each other as we wait for the elevator. There are no words. Just a few tears as the doors open and he slips inside. I wait until the doors close, wipe my eyes and head back into Sean's room.

A few minutes later, the nurse comes back with her little handheld device and a test strip. Once again, she sticks his finger and draws blood, but she smiles as the number appears, so I'm assuming it's in a better range because there is no shot this time. She lets me know the chair unfolds into a bed and she will bring me a blanket and pillow. She also tells us there's a playroom down the hall and we are welcome to go enjoy it.

As soon as Sean finishes his game, we go explore the playroom — a massive room with ping-pong tables, TVs with gaming consoles, board games, puzzles, couches and bean bag chairs spread around the space. Eyes wide, we smile at each other. "Where should we start?" I ask him. Ping-pong wins, followed by a board game and finally, bowling through the Wii gaming console. For an hour, we almost forget where we are, and as we agree to one more game, I take the opportunity to have a mental health check-in while he sets us up.

"So, how are you doing, honey?"

He stays focused on the screen and shrugs his shoulders.

"Do you have any questions or is there anything you want to talk about?"

"Not really." Then he turns to me with a very serious face. "Diabetes feels like a bully."

"In what way?"

"It won't go away, and it's always mean to you."

I stare at him, speechless. My heart hurts so much for him.

"I get it. I can see how it would feel that way." I wish I had words of wisdom to share with him, but in the moment, I agree with him and decide to just validate his feelings and move on.

Another hour later, the nurse comes to tell us she needs us to return to Sean's room. It's time to check his blood sugar again and take another insulin shot. We clean up and walk hand-in-hand back to his room.

Once again, Sean rises to the challenge. He doesn't say a word as they test his blood sugar with that little test strip or when they draw the insulin out of the little vial and give him a shot. He changes into his pajamas, brushes his teeth and crawls into bed. As I tuck him in, I pray tomorrow will be a better day for him. Exhausted, he falls asleep quickly.

I glance down at my phone and notice more missed calls and messages, which I listen to, but I can't muster up the energy or desire to call anyone back. Feeling depleted, with no ability to explain to anyone how much our lives changed over the last twelve hours, I plug my phone into the charger, grab my toiletries and get ready for bed. After unfolding the chair/bed and shaking out the blanket, I turn off the lights, lie down and stare up at the ceiling. My legs begin to shake and my eyes fill again as I try to picture what tomorrow will be like, but I can't see or feel anything other than an overwhelming fear. *How am I going to take care of him? How am I going to give him shots? I'm not qualified to do this.* Trying to focus on my breathing, I close my eyes, but sleep evades me.

As soon as the sun rises, I grab my clothes, and make my way to the bathroom. After a quick shower, I put on some makeup and stare at myself in the mirror. I look awful. The concealer I apply is no match for the puffiness around my eyes or the bags under them from not sleeping. I gather all my things, take a deep breath, and step out of the bathroom just as the day nurse is entering the room.

"Good morning, Mrs. Greene. Are you all ready to check out?" Staring at her, I try to comprehend what she just asked me. *Am I ready to check out?* As if this is a hotel and we are guests by choice. I shake my head, shrug my shoulders, and then, feeling rude, try to smile at her as I quietly pack our things while she gives Sean his insulin shot, and he eats breakfast.

The car ride to the endocrinologist's office is very quiet. I pull into a space and glance up at him through the rear-view mirror. He is staring out the window and I get this sinking feeling that this is his last moment of innocence. Reality is waiting to greet us right through those sliding glass doors.

Ten

David is waiting for us as we enter the building. He high-fives Sean and kisses me on the cheek. Sean tells David all about the game room we discovered as we find our way to the endocrinologist's office, where the receptionist hands me a stack of papers on a clipboard, along with a pen. After all the forms are completed, I return them to the receptionist and immediately, the side door in the waiting room opens and a petite woman, studying a paper she is holding, very officially and a little too loudly calls, "Sean Greene." I find this odd, since we are the only ones there at seven a.m. If I were watching this on TV I would have laughed, but nothing about today is funny to me.

We follow her through the door, where she checks Sean's height and weight and then leads us into an exam room. Sean hops up onto the table while David and I take the two seats waiting for us and, after telling us the doctor will be in shortly, she closes the door behind her.

A few minutes later, Dr. Aronson walks in. He is older than I expected. If I had to guess, I would say early sixties. He has gray hair, a kind face, and a slight frame. He puts his hand out toward Sean and says, "Hi. I'm Dr.

Aronson." Sean shakes his hand and introduces himself. Then he turns to us and repeats the introduction before turning back to Sean.

"So, Sean, do you know why you're here today?"

"The doctor in the hospital said I have diabetes. Is that true?" he asks, with a little quiver in his voice.

Dr. Aronson sits down facing our son. I'm impressed with the way he talks to him directly and can't help but wonder how many times a day he has this conversation.

"Unfortunately, Sean, it is true. You have type 1 diabetes. Your immune system is attacking cells in your pancreas that produce insulin. Our bodies need insulin to control our blood sugar. Your pancreas is not working properly and cannot produce insulin. When our blood sugars get too high, it hurts the other organs in our body. So the way we treat this is to give you insulin." He pauses to let this sink in.

"So if I take a shot of insulin it'll fix my pancreas?"

"Well, it'll help for a little while. Whenever you eat something with carbohydrates, you'll have to take a shot of insulin. Carbohydrates raise our blood sugar and insulin brings it down. If your pancreas was working, it would automatically release the insulin when you eat. But since yours doesn't, you will have to take a shot with every meal and snack." Again, he pauses.

Sean just stares at him. I see the tears he blinks away as he nods his head. I'm fighting tears myself.

Dr. Aronson examines Sean and then turns to us. He smiles a soft, apologetic smile and says, "He will do great. Denise, our diabetes educator, will meet with you shortly to teach you everything you need to know. Hang in there and call me anytime you need me." With an encouraging nod he leaves us alone, and we all sit staring straight ahead. There are no words. Just tears we all fight to control.

A few minutes pass and Denise walks into the room, introduces herself, and asks us to follow her to a drab, cramped meeting room, where we sit around a table covered with syringes, alcohol swabs and some other items I'm not familiar with. She hands us each a packet with big bold letters on the cover that says, "HOW TO MANAGE TYPE 1 DIABETES." With trembling hands, I turn the page.

For the next three hours we try to absorb as much as we can. Denise talks continuously about blood sugar control, monitoring Sean's blood sugar, long-acting and short-acting insulin, how to draw insulin from a vial into a syringe. She teaches us how to use a blood glucose meter to test Sean's blood sugar by inserting a test strip into a small, hand-held machine and drawing blood from his finger onto the strip, just like they did in the hospital. Denise encourages us to use our new machine right then and there, but Sean doesn't want to prick his finger himself, so David leans over and does it for him. He gently sticks the side of his finger and then places Sean's finger by the test strip. The tip of the test strip fills with blood and in ten seconds we have a number on the face of the machine. It reads 120 and Denise is pleased. It feels like we just passed a test.

I'm on information overload and completely over-whelmed, praying I can handle this, when she takes out a syringe, a vial of insulin — filled with water for practice purposes — and a rubber ball and places one set in front of each of us.

"And now we practice," she informs us.

Denise picks up her own vial and alcohol swab. She shows us how to wipe down the top of the vial and insert the syringe to draw out insulin. When she encourages us to tap the syringe to release any air bubbles, I flick at my syringe so hard I think it's going to crack. Then she shows us how to inject the insulin into the rubber ball. "Hold it just like a dart and quickly insert and push down on the plunger, then withdraw. Simple!"

Ha! Simple for her, maybe. But it isn't a ball I'll be jabbing multiple times a day. This is my son, real-life flesh and blood. Who in their right mind thought I could do this? And then I look across the table into Sean's eyes. They are as huge as saucers and filling quickly with tears, so I reach across the table and grab his hand. "We've got this, buddy. Don't you worry." And for that split second, I believe it too. David is quiet, practicing with his syringe and ball. Denise asks Sean if he wants to try it himself, but he shakes his head no and looks down at his lap. She reassures him that there is plenty of time for him to learn to give himself shots and for now, Mom and Dad will do a great job.

Denise reviews with us the log sheet that we will have to fill out and fax to her daily that will track Sean's blood sugars, amount of carbs eaten and the amount of insulin we give him, along with the time of injection. We are instructed to test his blood sugar when he wakes up and goes to sleep, before meals and snacks and then at midnight and three a.m. She assures me the midnight/three a.m. routine won't last too long but says, "we must watch carefully to make sure he is getting the correct amount of insulin. A low blood sugar, especially at night, could be dangerous." She also reviews the formulas we use to calculate his insulin for meals and at bedtime. Denise reminds us that everything is written in the packet, and we can always call her with any questions.

"Night or day, we are here for you," she assures me with a smile, as she hands over a large paper bag full of supplies to get us started, including a new vial of insulin and syringes. She hands David the prescriptions we have to fill and a recommendation for glucose tablets to treat low blood sugars.

Denise walks us out to the front desk and asks the receptionist to schedule our next appointment in a week.

Then, with a quick smile and a pat on my arm, she says, "You will be ok." Before I can answer, she turns and disappears through the door, and we are left alone.

Eleven

Sean and I drive home while David goes to fill our prescriptions. The minute we walk in the door, Sean runs into the kitchen and starts going through the pantry to find a snack. "I'm so hungry," he says.

He decides on a grilled cheese sandwich with chips and a cookie. I'm worried about the cookie, but Denise emphasized that he could eat what he wants as long as we count the carbs. I stare at the little vial of insulin on my kitchen counter, trying to make peace with the knowledge that this medication is what will keep my son alive. Too much or too little could kill him, and the burden of that responsibility is weighing heavily on me. I begin filling the syringe when my hands start to shake, and my chest constricts; it feels as if I can't breathe. Reaching, I hold the counter as I steady myself and focus on inhaling and exhaling. I'm giving myself a pep talk when I hear the door open. David calls, "Where is everyone?" and with a sigh of relief, I yell back that we're in the kitchen.

David joins us, carrying several bags of supplies, and quickly realizes what we are about to do. He kisses my forehead, places the bags on the counter and grabs an alcohol swab. Then he sits down next to Sean as I prepare his first injection, gently wiping down Sean's arm while he starts a conversation about the Panthers' upcoming football season. I walk over to Sean and kneel at eye level. "Ready, buddy?" He nods and David keeps talking to him as I quickly give him his first shot. "All done!" I say, as I smooth out his sleeve. "Eat up, Sean."

Sean digs into his lunch and I step quietly out of the kitchen, walking in a daze to my room, where I sit on the edge of my bed as tears glide down my face. Sean handled the shot so well. It didn't seem to hurt him. But the pain in my heart is unbearable.

Later that afternoon I make two phone calls, the first of which is to Ellen. I let her know I won't be back in to work until next Monday. She is very understanding and reassures me that I can take as much time as I need. Next, I call Melanie and let her know that Sean will be back in camp tomorrow. The doctor and Denise insisted that the best thing to do was go back to our "normal" routine. As if we will ever feel normal again. Melanie is excited to have him back. She says Billy and Cory keep asking for him.

"It's not fun for them if Sean isn't there. You can't be The Three Musketeers if one of the musketeers is missing." I can hear the smile in her voice, which warms me as I tell her we will see her in the morning. I listen to my messages and realize I've missed multiple calls from

Sherry and Karen along with my sister, brother and my mom and dad. I decide I only have the strength for one call, so I call my mom.

As soon as I hear her voice I start to cry. Through my sobs I describe our "new normal" to her. She listens without interrupting, which is a tremendous display of restraint on her part. When I finally finish going on about how sad and scared I am, she waits a moment and then asks, "Are you sure we can't come help you?" I so appreciate the offer, but I reassure her I am ok for now. Tasking her with updating my sister and brother, I hang up.

David and I agree that he will take the midnight shift and I will take the three a.m. blood sugar check. By the time we crawl into bed we are exhausted and in a matter of seconds David is out cold, while I am flat on my back, staring up at the ceiling. As tired as I am, I can't seem to fall asleep. Tears are streaming down my face, and I wonder if I will ever truly feel joy again. I'm trying to process my feelings, which right now amount to a ball of anger and immense sadness. My little boy's childhood has just been taken away from him. Gone are the carefree days. Now we are faced with constant finger sticks, constant monitoring, constant shots. My pantry shelf, once full of snacks and goodies, is now lined with endless medical supplies. I am chilled and hot at the same time. This has got to be a mistake. How did life change so drastically overnight?

My tears finally stop, but I am still restless. Just before midnight, I turn off David's alarm. No need for both of us to be up. I grab the meter and test strip, along with the little gadget that sticks his finger, and make my way down the hall to Sean's room. He is fast asleep, so I grab a small flashlight from the hall closet and stick the side of his little pinky. He doesn't even flinch. The meter registers 105. Perfect! I gather my things and tiptoe out of his room. Relieved that for the moment all is well, I slip back into bed and try to sleep. I must have dozed off because the three a.m. alarm wakes me. I jump out of bed and grab my little bag of supplies and repeat my twelve a.m. routine. This time the meter says sixty-five. UGH. His blood sugar is low. I run to the kitchen and grab a juice box. Back in his room, I gently wake Sean and tell him he has to drink some juice. He struggles to open his eyes and finally sits up and drinks. Once he finishes, he goes right back to sleep as I turn to see David in the doorway.

"Is there anything I can do?"

"Fix this."

He looks so sad. "I wish I could."

"Me too. Go back to sleep. I've got this."

Lying on the floor, I wait the instructed fifteen to twenty minutes before retesting Sean's blood sugar. He is back up in a normal range, so I leave him to sleep and head back to my room.

Twelve

The next morning, I pull into the camp parking lot and walk Sean in so I can go over a few things with Melanie and leave backup supplies in her office. I make it a few steps up the walkway when I hear, "Jessie...wait for us." I turn to see Sherry and Karen jogging to catch up as Billy and Cory run toward Sean. When they meet up, they high-five each other.

"You're back!'

"Camp was lame without you yesterday!"

"We get to play kickball today!"

The Three Musketeers are talking over each other as they head into camp.

Sherry gives me a side hug and Karen catches her breath as she asks how we are doing. Melanie has filled them in, so I don't have to relive the story. As soon as I feel Sherry's arm around me, I tear up. Oh my God. I have to stop this. My emotions are so raw right now. I swallow, take a deep breath and squeak out, "I'm ok." But she doesn't believe me.

"Do you want to meet for lunch?" asks Karen. "We can circle back around noon."

I give her a weak smile and shake my head. "I have to

be back here at lunchtime to test his blood sugar and give him insulin. Maybe another time?"

"Of course. Whenever you want," says Sherry with a little squeeze.

I drop off a few bottles of glucose tablets for low blood sugars, along with the test kit he will need to check his blood sugar. I promise to be back before lunch and Melanie promises to call me with any questions.

Heading straight to the gym, I take out all my frustrations on the elliptical machine. An hour later I am drained and sweaty and feeling a little lighter. With two hours to go until lunch, I decide to run home and take a quick shower but immediately turn the car around when I start to panic. *What if Melanie calls and needs me?* Making my way back to the camp parking lot, I find a shaded spot toward the back and roll the windows down. I use the time to catch up on calls with my family until it's time for lunch. Melanie is waiting for me, and we chat a little before the counselor brings Sean in. He is carrying his lunch and looks a little flushed. He sits down and we test his blood sugar. Thirty-Five. Oh no...way too low and too scary for me. I grab the bottle of glucose tables and take a few out, break one in half and hand it to Sean.

He looks at it and shakes his head. "I don't want it."

I take a deep breath, kneel to his eye level, and in a low, steady voice I barely recognize I say, "Sweetheart, I understand, but we have no choice."

He blinks a few times, takes the tablet out of my hand, and slowly starts to chew. Glucose tablets are big and chalky and gross, but he chews all four and then sits there, staring at me, while Melanie runs to the kitchen to get him some water to wash it down. I sit down next to him and gently rub his back until Melanie returns with the water, which Sean gulps down as we quietly watch the clock, waiting to retest. Hearing a commotion in the hallway, Melanie steps outside her office to watch over the campers as they make their way into the lunchroom. Anger starts bubbling up inside of me. Sean should be running into lunch with his friends. Not sitting here pale and sweating, waiting for his blood sugar to stabilize. Finally, the time passes, and his blood sugar rises to a good range. He grabs his lunch, gives me a quick hug and I watch him as he sprints into the lunchroom and claims his seat between Billy and Cory.

Back home, I make a few calls to confirm final details for Friday night's welcome service and reception. It dawns on me as I hang up the phone with the rabbi that I'm dreading Friday night. I used to love going to services as a family, always enjoying the fellowship and relishing the way the Shabbat service soothed my soul. Our synagogue always felt like home to me. Now, nothing feels normal and quite frankly I am just so angry at God. I look up at the sky and shake my head. It's not fair. Kids should be off-limits. They shouldn't get cancer, they shouldn't get autism and they shouldn't get diabetes. As a matter of fact, nothing bad should ever happen to children. They should be allowed to be kids. What kind of God lets this happen? And therein lies my struggle with Friday night. Because as angry as I am, I know come Friday, I will put on a dress, paste a smile on my face and we will go to synagogue. Because that's what we do.

When the dreaded Friday night arrives, logistically everything goes according to plan. The pews are so full you would think it was a holiday. I follow along with the service but lose my focus and find myself wondering what it all means. The prayers I've said my entire life have suddenly lost meaning to me. What's the point to all of this? Nothing about this is soothing my soul. I close the prayer book, sit back, and wait for the service to end.

During the reception Sherry, Karen and I huddle in a back corner. These women are my chosen sisters. We met in Mommy and Me classes when our babies were three months old and bonded as boys' moms raising only children. When the boys were ready for religious school, we all joined the synagogue together. I'd be lost without them.

Sherry reminds us that in two weeks we will be celebrating Karen's birthday in Nashville. It's all we've thought about for the last few months. The plan is to fly into Nashville on a Friday morning and fly home on Sunday. As they ramble on about what time we should leave for the airport and the restaurants they want to try before hitting the clubs on Broadway I become anxious. *Can I be that far away from Sean? What about his midnight blood checks? I'm always there for that. What if something goes wrong and David needs me?* I stay quiet as they hash out the details. We had planned our girls' weekend long before all this happened. When we made our plans, I was so excited. Now I'm just anxious and nervous.

Later that night I remind David about Nashville.

"I'm not sure I should go. Maybe I can get a refund for my airline tickets," I say over my shoulder as I change for bed.

"Why would you do that?"

"Because I'll be a plane ride away. I don't know if I can be that far away right now."

"I can't think of one good reason why you should cancel. You've been so excited about this trip. I don't want you to miss it. Go have a good time. I'll be here and if I need help, I can call the doctor's office."

"But..."

"No buts, Jessie. We can't stop living. Sean has to see that diabetes will not stand in the way of anything we want to do, and your staying home does not send that message. We have to set an example."

I stay quiet and think about what he says. I know he's right. It's me. I'm afraid to be away from Sean. Afraid if I take my eyes off him, something bad will happen.

Thirteen

Sitting in a plane on my way to Nashville with my two closest friends I listen to them laughing about something funny that happened at yoga class. I'm quiet, trying to relax and enjoy the fact that for the next two days I have no responsibilities. As soon as we arrive, I step aside to call David. He assures me they are doing great. Sean gets on the phone and tells me to have fun.

The energy in Nashville is off the charts. After we check into the hotel and grab a bite to eat, we make our way down Broadway. Squeezing through the crowd into the iconic Tootsie's, Karen notices a group getting up to leave and she quickly grabs their seats. The band is taking requests, and someone yells out, "Me and Bobby McGee," so the band kicks in and we sing along with everyone else in the bar at the top of our lungs. After about an hour, we make our way out onto the street and continue bar-hopping. For the next two days, I live in an alternate universe where everything is light and fun, and I have no worries.

By Sunday morning, I'm feeling rejuvenated and overly eager to get home. We breeze through security and sing along with the live music throughout the concourse until we approach our gate and our phones start dinging with alerts from the airline. Apparently, our flight has been delayed thirty minutes. I call David to let him know. He reassures me there is nothing to worry about. He and Sean are having fun and will be at the airport to pick me up.

Thirty minutes later another alert comes across my phone. The flight is now delayed an additional hour. Sherry and Karen immediately see this as an opportunity to extend the party and want to head to the bar. I, on the other hand, am praying that any minute they are going to make an announcement that they are ready to board. I don't want to leave the gate, so I offer to stay with our things, and they eagerly take me up on the offer. Watching them from a distance, I notice that they are completely carefree, easily laughing at something the bartender says as he hands them their drinks. I envy them, and, becoming increasingly agitated, I walk over to the gate attendant. She has no new information, so I sit down and call David. We chat and catch up a little bit, but it's lunch time there and he needs to go help Sean, leaving me with a pit in my stomach, feeling guilty for not being there checking his blood sugar and giving him his insulin.

Two hours later I'm pacing back and forth by our things as I watch Karen and Sherry entertain other travelers with stories from our weekend. Finally, they return to the gate. Karen turns to me and, in a tone I interpret as very patronizing and dismissive, says, "Jessie, you do know that pacing back and forth will not make the plane leave any sooner. Relax." And then she has the audacity to roll her eyes at me.

I glare at her, trying to decide if I should tell her to shut up or defend myself. Ultimately, I continue to pace, and they continue to party. There is nothing in my control right now, so I know I have to let it go, but I'm so annoyed. Finally, the girl behind the desk announces that we are ready to board. Again, Karen looks me in the eye. "Happy now?"

The sarcasm is evident. It's not unlike Karen to act this way when she drinks too much, but I can't help feeling hurt. Ignoring her, I call David to give him our ETA and get in line to board.

Fourteen

Over the next few weeks, we have our ups and downs, but we are getting the hang of our new routine. I'm starting to crave some normalcy, so I ask Karen and Sherry if they want to drop Cory and Billy off for a playdate on Saturday. Karen has family coming to visit but Sherry is all in. She drops off Billy mid-afternoon and we arrange for her and her husband Richard to come back later for dinner. Looking forward to a fun night, I order the pizzas and have just finished tossing the salad when the doorbell rings and David yells, "I've got it." He walks our guests into the kitchen, opens a bottle of wine, and we toast to good friends and clink glasses just as Billy comes running into the kitchen.

"Mrs. Greene, Sean doesn't feel so good."

I grab the meter and test strips and head to the playroom. Sure enough, he is low — too much fun, not enough food — so I give him some glucose tablets and Billy joins us as we sit and wait for Sean's blood sugar to come up. I look up to see Sherry standing in the doorway. She has a look of pity on her face that she quickly hides with a timid smile. I smile back at her and make light of it. "He's great." I tell her. "Just a little too much fun! Pizza should be here soon." After we retest and confirm he is ok, Sherry and I head back toward the kitchen. Luckily, the pizza arrives and the commotion of everyone grabbing plates and drinks allows me and Sean a chance to quietly step away. After calculating his carbs and quickly giving him his insulin shot, we rejoin everyone before they realize we were gone. At least, I think they didn't realize. I feel a little uneasy and suddenly find myself not wanting to draw too much attention to this. I want them to see Sean as Sean, and not as Sean with T1D.

Fifteen

On a sunny Thursday in July, Sean and I are on our way to Dr. Aronson's office for his one-month check-up. He's grumpy because he will be late for camp. We pull into the parking lot, and I look at Sean through the rearview mirror.

"Ready, buddy?" I ask, trying to sound cheerful.

"I hate diabetes," he whispers as he unbuckles his seatbelt.

"Me, too!" I whisper back, never taking my eyes off him in the mirror.

"I hate it more," he says a little louder.

"I hate diabetes more!" I say even louder.

We go back and forth getting louder and louder yelling "I hate diabetes" over and over until we both start laughing.

"If anyone hears us, they'll think we're nuts, but that sure felt good."

"It sure did," Sean says, still chuckling.

Then we both get out of the car and walk into the office.

After dropping him off at camp, I meet Sherry and Karen for lunch. It's been a while since we've been able to spend time, just the three of us. Between running to camp every day at lunchtime and working three days a week, I don't have much time to meet friends. The conversation flows easily, and we laugh and chat until the tables around us empty out and we rise to leave. For the first time in a little over a month, I have not thought about or talked about diabetes, and it feels great!

As we are walking out of the restaurant I ask, "What time are you guys coming over on Sunday?"

There's a very awkward pause before Sherry says, "I don't think we're going to be around this Sunday. Sorry to miss our pool day. "

Karen immediately chimes in with, "We aren't available this Sunday either. Next week for sure!" She jumps in her car and waves before I can respond.

I'm a little surprised that they both have plans. Sundays have always been our day to get our families together. I ignore the strange feeling in my gut and tell myself it's summer and everyone is busy. I know there are times one of us has to bow out, but it seems a little odd that they both have plans for Sunday and didn't elaborate on what they were.

Driving home, I start thinking about our lunch conversation and realize we spent a lot of time talking about everything but the kids, which is unusual for us. And I can't shake the feeling that something is up with this weekend. I'm starting to get an uneasy feeling in my stomach but can't really place my finger on what is bothering me. At dinner I tell David about it, and he thinks it's odd too.

"Probably just a coincidence. Let's take advantage of it and get away for the weekend. We can go to Atlanta tomorrow, visit the aquarium and do some shopping. It'd be nice to have a change of scenery," he offers as we clear the plates from the table.

As I make a list of all the supplies I need to bring with us for Sean, I find it mind-boggling how much stuff we need to take for an overnight getaway. David makes us a hotel reservation and Sean seems excited about our spontaneous adventure.

We start out right after breakfast. It's a two-hour drive with no traffic, so we go straight to the aquarium, where we spend several hours walking through the exhibits before we make our way to the exit. When Sean says he feels "funny," we stop to test his blood sugar, which is low from all the walking. But after he eats some glucose tablets, plus a snack, and is feeling better, we pile into the car and head to The Varsity. It's our favorite burger joint and we can't visit Atlanta without stopping there for lunch. We round out the afternoon by shopping for some school clothes at Phipps Plaza. By the time we check into the hotel, we are all exhausted. This trip was exactly what we needed.

Sixteen

The following Monday, Sean comes home from camp and seems a little out of sorts. When I ask him how his day was, he just shrugs. He doesn't want to talk much, so he grabs a book and lies down on the couch in the family room. I keep an eye on him while I make dinner. When we sit down to eat, David tries to engage him in conversation, but Sean gives one-word answers, causing David to look across the table at me with raised eyebrows as I shrug my shoulders. It's game night, and in the middle of playing parchesi, Sean sits back in his chair and announces, "I don't want to play anymore."

"What's going on, champ?" asks David.

"Nothing."

"Something is bothering you, and in our family, we don't keep secrets so spill your guts, man."

Sean looks up with tears in his eyes. He looks back and forth between us and then looks down at his lap.

"Billy and Cory went to that big waterpark in Charlotte for the weekend. They said I couldn't go because I have diabetes."

My blood starts to boil. What the heck! Seriously?

We've all been friends since these boys were babies and they plan a trip to the waterpark and don't invite us? We've talked about taking that trip as a group. How could they? I am so upset, and my heart hurts once again for Sean.

David leans over and takes Sean's hand. "Are you sure that's what they said?"

Sean nods as tears start to fall.

I get up, make my way to his seat and wrap my arms around him, holding him tight. I'm looking over his head at David and can see by the expression on his face that he is as shocked and as angry as I am. But right now we have to push that aside because our little man is hurting.

I pull away and softly place my hands on his face so he is looking right at me. He tries to turn away, but I gently say, "Look at me, Sean."

He turns his head back toward mine.

"Listen to me closely. There is absolutely nothing you can't do. You are Sean Greene. The same boy you were before you got diabetes. Diabetes is something you have. It is not who you are."

David chimes in. "You are still the same boy who loves football and basketball and Legos and collecting cars and playing with your friends. Your routine changed. YOU DID NOT!"

Sean looks like he is starting to believe us, but then turns to David and asks, "Then why didn't they want me to go with them?"

"Sean, sometimes people get scared when they don't have all the facts. They assume things instead of asking. But that is about them, not about you. I know it hurts to be left out, but this is on them. Not on you."

He nods, hugs us, and says he is tired and wants to go to bed.

As we tuck him in, I kiss his forehead and tell him I love him. David does the same and as we turn out the light, David takes my hand and we walk to our bedroom so we can talk without Sean overhearing us.

As soon as the door closes, I explode. "What is wrong with Sherry and Karen? I thought they were our friends. How could they do that to him? Did they think their boys wouldn't tell Sean about their weekend? Why didn't they ask me if he could go and just assume he couldn't?"

David lets me rant and when I exhaust myself, he pulls me close and just holds me as my eyes overflow with the emotions I try so hard to suppress.

The next morning, I bring Sean to camp. After a good night's sleep, he seems more like himself and is excited about the dance party they are having that afternoon. I drop him off, remind him I will see him at lunch and go straight to the gym. Throughout my entire workout I debate with myself over whether-or-not to say something to Sherry and Karen. In the end, I decide to let it go. We resume our Sunday get-togethers, and everything seems ok, although, since the waterpark incident, I feel a little self-conscious around them when we check Sean's blood sugar or give him insulin. At the same time, I want Sean to feel as comfortable as possible taking care of himself and don't want him to feel the stigma of T1D or think it's something he has to hide, so I keep my feelings to myself.

The last week of July, Sherry calls to invite Sean to Billy's birthday party the following Wednesday night. They are taking a group of Billy's friends out to dinner at his favorite restaurant. I glance at my calendar and realize I have a synagogue board meeting that night.

"I can drop Sean off, but David will have to pick him up after dinner because I have a board meeting at seven o'clock."

"Really? I was hoping you would stay with us for dinner."

"That is so sweet to include me, but I can't miss this meeting."

"You can't miss one meeting? Or maybe stay for dinner and be a little late for the meeting?"

It's not like Sherry to put so much pressure on me. Between her and Karen, it's usually Sherry who offers to take Sean on outings with her family, but it's clear to me now that she does not want me to drop Sean off. I'm not sure what's going on but I don't want a confrontation so I give in and tell her I will stay, and David will meet me to bring Sean home so I can go to the meeting after dinner.

I hang up with a sinking feeling in my stomach. Sherry used to take Sean with them all the time, but now that I think about it, she hasn't offered to have him over since he was diagnosed.

That night after Sean goes to sleep, I tell David about our conversation, sharing with him that I am so agitated I'm at a loss for how to approach this, because the bottom line is, if she is not comfortable with my child anymore, there is nothing I can do to change her feelings. I've tried to share our routine with her, make her and Karen a part of things so they would feel comfortable, but they show no interest, other than their superficial, "How are you? How is he coping?" It's not that they aren't supportive, it's just not in the way I need them to be. Because what I really need is for them to act the way they did before T1D, yet my gut is telling me those days are long gone.

Seventeen

At the beginning of August, we receive the name of Sean's fourth grade teacher. I call the school to schedule our appointment to review our 504 plan, which details how the school will handle situations that arise regarding his diabetes. Sean and I go to the school and spend an hour educating his teacher, the school counselor, the nurse, and the principal about T1D. We are all in agreement that Sean will go to the nurse before lunch to test his blood sugar and get his insulin shot. At any point during the day if he doesn't feel well, he can check his blood sugar in class, but if he is low or high, a classmate will accompany him to the nurse's office. Most importantly, he will be excused from any standardized testing if his blood sugar is above 250 or below seventy-five as this can impact his ability to concentrate and could have far-reaching implications regarding his education if he does not perform well under these circumstances.

Sean is bursting with enthusiasm following his first day of school, and barely closes the car door as he tells me about his new friend Noah Whitman, who just moved here from California. Sean wants to invite him over this weekend, so I look over the class list and, finding Noah's home phone number, call his mom, Abby. After a few minutes of small talk, I invite Noah over on Saturday for a playdate, which Abby really appreciates, since they are still unpacking from their move. We agree she will drop Noah off at noon, and as we hang up, I catch a glimmer of my old self. I am so happy for Sean that he has a new friend, and hopeful for me that maybe I'll have a new friend too.

Friday, I'm at my desk, bogged down with paperwork, when I glance at the clock and realize if I don't leave work immediately, I will be late for my monthly lunch date with Sherry and Karen. I leave a stack of resumés on Ellen's desk with a summary of my observations and hurry to my car. Pulling up to the restaurant, I see Sherry and Karen sitting at a table through the window and take a moment to observe. They look so serious as they lean in toward each other, deep in conversation. Taking a deep breath, I walk into the restaurant and as I approach the table, they stop talking and smile up at me. We air kiss hello and after ordering lunch, we catch up on synagogue gossip. Religious school will start soon, and with that our Sunday routine of class, followed by lunch at one of our houses so the kids can play. Since our boys go to different elementary schools, during the school year their only chance to get together is Sunday afternoons. When I ask where we should meet this Sunday, they both start to answer at the same time, then laugh awkwardly before Karen asks if we can just meet at my house. Apparently, Karen's husband has a big project for work and is spending Sunday preparing. Sherry never offers to host at her house. I agree to my house but, again, something feels uncomfortable. Gone is the ease we used to have with each other.

Saturday can't come fast enough for Sean. He runs through the house to answer the door as soon as the doorbell rings. I follow closely behind him and am greeted by a beautiful blond woman with long hair, blue eyes, and the kindest, friendliest smile I've seen in a long time. I return the smile and wish I had worn something a little nicer than my faded jean shorts and Springsteen concert T-shirt. Way to make a first impression! Noah is cute as can be and very polite. After the introductions, the boys run off to Sean's playroom and Abby and I make small talk trying to get to know one another. I offer to drop Noah off at their house before dinner and Abby thanks me again before she leaves.

David gathers the boys, and we take them for lunch before driving to the Fun Park to play mini-golf. When Sean's blood sugar goes low and he needs a break to eat some glucose tablets, Noah doesn't miss a beat. He sits on the bench with Sean, talking about his friends in California and asking Sean school questions until he feels ready to continue playing. On the way home we stop for ice cream and while David takes Noah to the window to order, I give Sean insulin to cover the cone he's about to eat. The boys laugh and tell corny jokes while we eat trying to top each other with the silliest stories. When we arrive at Noah's house, Abby answers the door and after thanking us for a fun day says, "Next playdate is on us," as she waves goodbye.

I'm still riding a wave of joy from our weekend when David calls from work to say he isn't feeling well and has excruciating pain in his back, which seemed to come out of nowhere. He called the doctor, who suggested he go to the ER. One of his co-workers offers to drive him there and I assure him I will drop Sean off at Karen or Sherry's and meet him there shortly. When I reach Sherry and tell her what is happening, she stutters a little as she explains that she is heading out the door for an appointment and is so sorry, but she can't help us. I call Karen but apparently, she also has an appointment and is sorry she isn't available. I grab Sean's back-up supply kit, add a few snacks, stuff a book in his backpack with his homework and take him with me. We sit in the ER for five hours. I try calling Karen and Sherry a few hours into our wait, but neither picks up the phone.

The doctor runs every test they can think of and surprises us when they determine he has kidney stones. They give him medicine for the pain and instructions on how to care for himself and finally release him. By the time we get home it's late, so I give Sean a light dinner and he goes to sleep.

After turning off the lights and locking up the house, I walk into our bedroom, where David is lying in bed watching TV. He looks exhausted. The pain meds are working, and he seems more comfortable, so I crawl in bed beside him, kiss him gently and lay my head on his chest.

He asks me what happened with Karen and Sherry. I tell him how hurt I am that when I tried to drop Sean off, they weren't available. We've always been there for each other, and I can't help but feel let down. When they both call later that night to check on David, I tell them it's kidney stones, that he'll be ok, but I really don't have time to talk. We are both so tired.

The next day I am cleaning out the closet when the phone rings. It is Abby calling to invite Sean over for a playdate on Saturday. I take a deep breath, brace myself and say, "Thank you so much for the invite. Before I accept, I need to tell you that Sean has type 1 diabetes. He carries a bag with him that has everything he needs, and he is good about testing his blood sugar and usually can tell when it's low." I pause, afraid to scare her off, not sure if I am saying too much or not saying enough when Abby interrupts me before I can continue.

"Jessie, my dad had type 1 diabetes and there were many times I had to help him, so there is no need to worry. Sean is safe in our house."

My tears are falling so fast, I have to take a moment before I can respond. It's amazing how much I have cried in the last few months.

"Abby, thank you so much. Sean would love to come over Saturday."

"Jessie, I should also mention that I have given my dad insulin shots before and if I had to, I can do the same for Sean. You just have to tell me how much insulin he gets before a meal. I promise you he will be in good hands here."

"I can't tell you how much that means to me." We make plans, and I hang up and sob. Finally, someone who isn't afraid to be around my son without me there.

Eighteen

At the end of September we have our three-month endocrinology follow-up with Dr. Aronson. David and I both take the morning off work so we can all go together. Once we're in the examining room, they check Sean's blood sugar and his A1C, which gives them an average of how his blood sugar has been managed over the last three months. We are not waiting long when Dr. Aronson comes in, accompanied by Denise, the diabetes educator. Denise is carrying a device that resembles a pager with tubes protruding from one end, and as they sit down, Dr. Aronson takes the device from Denise.

"Hey, champ. How are you?" he asks Sean.

"I'm good. When can I stop taking these shots?" He asks this every time, always hoping the answer is now. It never is. It never will be. This is not going away.

"Well, I'm glad you asked me that today." He hands Sean the device and continues. "Sean, this is called an insulin pump. The way it works is that you fill this little reservoir at the end of this tube with insulin. Then you insert it in the case right here." He points to an opening on the pump. I can see that one side of the pump has buttons and a small display window. Dr. Aronson continues, "This pump will give you your insulin. We will input your carb rations so the pump will release the right amount of insulin based on the amount of carbs you eat, and it also delivers a background insulin drip twenty-four hours a day, which we call a basal rate. After you fill the reservoir and prime the tube, you take this end with the needle, and you place it on your stomach, where it can stay for three days. If you wear this, you won't have to take shots throughout the day. It's just one stick every two to three days instead of multiple shots a day."

Denise shows us that the little metal needle is surrounded by adhesive, while explaining that once you insert it through the skin, it adheres to that spot. Insulin is released into the tube and delivered into the body through the needle, similar to an IV tube transporting fluid from the bag to the patient.

Sean is turning the pump over in his hand and examining the tubes. Then he focuses on the needle at the end of the tube and looks up at Denise with a worried expression. "Does this hurt?"

Denise assures him it's a little pinch just like the shots he gets. "With this insulin pump, you can enter your carbs right into the device, so you won't need Mom to come to school every day at lunchtime or to stay close by when you're at a friend's house." She looks at me and David and adds, "He can be more independent if he wears this."

My heart is pounding. I absolutely despise giving him his shots, but at least I have control. Turning over that control to a device is scary. *What if it malfunctions? What if it gives him too much insulin or too little? How do they know what settings will work for him?* My mind is buzzing with questions and I'm trying to decide which one to ask first when David asks, "Will this give us more control over his blood sugars?"

Dr. Aronson nods and says, "Yes, we are finding that patients on insulin pumps are able to lower their A1C's, and for the young ones, it gives them much more freedom. We start out conservatively with his settings, and once he gets used to wearing the pump, we make changes. You will keep a log like you did in the beginning with the time of day, his blood sugar and the amount of carbs he eats, and we will make adjustments according to his log sheets. You'll still need to test him at midnight and at three a.m. to make sure we get the settings correct, but, again, no more shots."

He looks over at Sean. "What do you think, Sean? Are you willing to give it a try?"

Sean looks at us and we smile at him. I'm still a little shaky about making a change but if it gives him a little bit of normalcy and eliminates the shots, I'm all for it. I nod yes and David nods yes and Sean looks at Dr. Aronson and says "Ok."

Of course, this is a process. Dr. Aronson's office will submit the paperwork to the insurance company and once it is approved, they will schedule a training session for us to come back and learn to use the pump.

Later that night, David and I talk about the pump and agree this may be a great way to care for Sean. I'm trying to get past the fact that my son will have a needle and tubes attached to him twenty-four-seven. We both realize this will be a tremendous adjustment for him. I tell David I wish we knew someone else with T1D who wears this pump. And then it dawns on me. Denise will know lots of kids wearing an insulin pump. Maybe she can introduce us to one of the families dealing with this too. David agrees I should call Denise first thing in the morning.

As soon as I drop Sean off at school, I rush home to call Denise. She is more than happy to help and says she has just the family in mind. She promises me she will contact the mom and ask permission to make the introduction and, true to her word, a few hours later she calls me back with a phone number for Valerie Walker. Not wasting any time, I call Valerie and we arrange to meet for coffee.

The next morning, I walk into the coffee shop and a petite brunette wearing yoga pants and an oversized T-shirt waves at me. I make my way to the table, and she immediately stands up and hugs me. She asks me what my drink of choice is and then goes to order for both of us. Returning to the table, Valerie hands me my coffee, leans across the table and says, "I hate diabetes." I immediately love her.

I smile back at her and say, "The feeling is mutual."

From there the conversation flows. We compare stories about the day our boys were diagnosed and find they are very similar. We both get angry when I describe how I locked eyes with Dr. Matheson across the parking lot as we were leaving for the hospital and how he had an "oops-I'm-sorry" look on his face, which made my blood boil, so that all I wanted to do was shout at him: "You missed this, you condescending, dismissive, lame excuse for a doctor." We shed a few tears when Valerie shares that they physically had to hold her son John down for his insulin shots and how, when she told the doctor she didn't think she could use force on her own child, he placed his hands on her shoulders, stared directly into her eyes and as gently as he could, said, "This is not using force to harm him. This is keeping him alive."

We compare notes about the friends who listen politely but then change the subject, and the ones who stopped inviting our kids to play at their house but are very willing to accept invitations to play at our homes. We moan about the sleep deprivation that comes from staying up until midnight and waking at three a.m. to check blood sugars. We share stories of those first few weeks, the shock and sorrow of the new reality our children are facing. Two hours and several cups of coffee later, we get up to leave and, as we are walking out the door, Valerie invites us over for dinner on Friday night. I thank her, write down her address and promise to bring dessert.

Sharing our conversation later that night with David, I tell him how much better I feel since coffee with Valerie. She explained it really well. She likens it to a death. The care-free childhood we counted on for our boys has died and we have to mourn that loss, which means experiencing all the stages of grief. I'm becoming very familiar with those stages: denial, anger, bargaining, depression, and the one that seems the hardest to achieve, acceptance. Every morning right before I open my eyes I think, *today I will wake from this nightmare.* But I don't. I walk around in a little bit of a fog. I go through the motions of the day and try to smile and laugh and find the joy, but very little makes me feel truly happy right now. The only time I am even a little bit like my old self is when the three of us are alone together. Then I don't feel like I have to pretend or hide or downplay the stress of worrying about Sean.

Nineteen

Friday night, armed with a tray of fruit and homemade sugar-free brownies, we drive to Valerie's house. She greets us at the door and introduces us to her husband Mike and son John. John and Sean hit it off right away. Mike and David recognize each other from the gym and their conversation flows as Mike hands David a beer and they step out into the backyard. Valerie and I make our way to the kitchen, where she hands me a glass of wine.

We chat as if we are old friends. I ask her how John is doing with the insulin pump. She says he is getting used to wearing a device all the time but it's not slowing him down. We are still waiting for the insurance approval but I'm feeling more optimistic about it now that I've met Valerie. Our conversation shifts to our families, and it feels like we've known each other much longer than a week.

It's amazing how at ease I am when Sean and John both come to dinner and pull out their meters to test their blood sugars. No stigma. No hiding. The only difference is that I fill a syringe and John pulls out his insulin pump and shows Sean how he enters his blood sugar and his carbs into the pump. The pump does all the calculations and releases insulin. So simple.

Sean asks if he can see the needle and John lifts his shirt to show him the white adhesive on his stomach with the tube leading to the pump. He answers all of Sean's questions and I listen to them discuss diabetes as David stands behind me and rubs my shoulders. Leaning into him, I realize I'm starting to feel hopeful. Witnessing John's ease with the pump is encouraging and I'm more excited than nervous now to give Sean back some of his independence.

Over dinner, Valerie asks if David and I have heard about Breakthrough T1D and, after shaking our heads, she tells us it's a non-profit organization focused on funding research to treat and cure type 1 diabetes. Their annual fundraiser, Walk To Cure T1D, is taking place at Simpson Park in November and she invites us to join their team. Mike suggests that Sean invite some friends too, and Valerie says she will send me a link to register our family. Just being with their family, I feel better.

Sunday afternoon, I'm still on a high from Friday night as Sherry, Karen and I are finishing lunch on my back deck while the boys are out front on the driveway playing basketball. I tell them about the walk at Simpson Park and they both seem excited and immediately say yes, so I give them the details before stepping inside the house to grab some water bottles. I'm about to step outside when I notice Karen and Sherry leaning in close and whispering. I hesitate for a minute and try to hear what they are talking about, but I can't, so as I approach them, I ask, "What's up? What am I missing?"

They both turn to me with a look of guilt on their faces. Sherry nods at Karen, who turns to me and says, "Jessie, I have to tell you something. I don't want you to be hurt but I don't want to hide things from you either."

I try to smile at her, but it feels forced. "Karen, we've been friends a long time. What's wrong?"

"Nothing is wrong. It's just, Cory's birthday is coming up and when we asked him what he wanted to do for his birthday he said he wants to bring some friends for an overnight trip to Atlanta for a hockey game."

She pauses and I patiently wait for her to continue. I anticipate she's about to ask if I would come with them and take a hotel room for me and Sean. I'm thinking through the logistics when she continues.

"We told him he could choose three friends. He chose two boys in his class and Billy. I'm so sorry, Jessie. You know we love Sean, but we can't take him with us." Then she sits back in her chair and just stares at me, obviously relieved that it's out in the open.

I'm speechless. I can't even process how I feel because my first thought is about Sean and how hurt he will be if he finds out they went without him. I lean forward in my chair and stare out at the backyard. I hear Sean in the kitchen, so

I excuse myself and check on my son. He is about to test his blood sugar and I watch as the meter displays fifty-five. He sits down at the table, and after giving him juice and a little snack, I sit down next to him. I love this boy more than I have ever loved anyone or anything in my life. And my heart hurts more than it ever has for him. When he retests, his number is in a great range, so he goes back outside to his friends, but I don't move. I look through the window onto my deck at my two friends. *How did things change so quickly? Did I misjudge them? Were we not as close as I thought we were? Or is this just too much for them to handle?*

Sherry comes inside and asks if everything is ok. I tell her everything is fine, but I need a minute. She goes back to sit with Karen and slowly I rise from the table, walk outside, and suggest that we wrap up this play date. Karen asks if I want to talk about it, but I shake my head no. I tell them I have a headache and need to lie down. Truthfully, I just want them to leave.

After they collect their things and the boys say goodbye, I suggest Sean go finish his homework. David is playing golf, so I go into our room and lie down on our bed. I close my eyes and let the tears stream down my face. Yes, I know. I cry a lot. My emotions are just so raw. I'm angry and I'm hurt. I felt the shift but somehow had hoped that we could repair it. Now I am starting to believe our friendship is not reparable. Too many let-downs and hurt feelings since Sean was diagnosed.

Twenty

Monday morning, as I walk into work, my phone rings. It's Noah's mom Abby calling to invite Sean over for a playdate Sunday afternoon. After hesitating for a minute, I accept the invitation and extend an invitation of my own for Abby and Noah to join us at the walk. Once I hang up, I wrestle with a little guilt for accepting a Sunday afternoon playdate, but quickly come to terms with the fact that I'm no longer obligated to Karen and Sherry. This change in routine is on them and they will have to explain it to their boys. I quickly type a text message letting them know we won't be available Sunday and then try my best to focus on work.

During our Monday morning meeting, I let Ellen know I will be out on Friday because we have an appointment to train for Sean's new pump. She doesn't look happy about it, but she nods and makes a note on her calendar. I'm not sure if I'm being overly sensitive or if she is getting tired of me asking for time off, but I internally commit to being as present as I can be when I'm in the office and don't leave my desk until it's time to pick up Sean.

Friday, I wake up a bundle of nerves, anxious about

changing our routine. I pray he will adjust well and that he won't have an issue with the needle insertion, while trying to wrap my head around the fact that he will have tubes attached to his body. I start pleading with the God I have lost faith in to please let this go well. *Please let it not hurt him. Please take this away from him. I'll do anything, give up anything, for this illness to go away.*

When we get to the office, Denise calls us back quickly, and we go to the room where they first trained us to give Sean shots. She takes out all the supplies and walks us through the mechanics of the pump. Showing us a list of settings, she begins to enter them while she explains what she is doing, assuring me that everything is outlined in the booklet she will give us before we leave. She works with Sean, practicing how to read various nutrition labels and how to enter the carb counts into the pump. Sean catches on quickly and she seems confident that he will do just fine.

When it's time to fill the reservoir with his insulin, Sean shakes his head no and folds his arms across his chest. I get the honors, and Denise demonstrates how to use the syringe that comes with the reservoir to draw the insulin out of the vial and inject it into the reservoir. Once that's done, we attach the tube and place the reservoir into the pump case. Then we hit a button and it primes the tube, allowing insulin to flow from the reservoir through the tube and out the little needle. When it drips with insulin the prime is over, and we can insert the needle in Sean's stomach. Denise instructs me to locate the two little plastic tabs that fold back like butterfly wings and use those to hold the needle straight. Just like with a syringe, the idea is to go in straight and quickly, then immediately press the adhesive to his skin. Sounds simple but I'm frozen and petrified.

David has already wiped Sean's stomach with an alcohol wipe and is holding his hand. Sean is staring at me.

I look to Denise, and she smiles at me. "You've got this, Jessie." Then she looks toward Sean. "Are you ready, Sean?"

He shakes his head no, so we give him a minute to prepare and then I realize I have to show him I'm ok.

"Let's get this done, Sean, so we can have a snack. On the count of three. Ready?" He nods and squeezes David's hand. I count "One.....two.....three," while I pinch up some skin with my left hand, using my right to insert the needle and smooth out the adhesive. Sean takes a deep breath and moves his fingers gently over the adhesive. He is staring at his stomach and I'm staring at him. He looks up and says, "I'm ok." I exhale and smile at him. We high-five and I say, "We've got this!"

Denise lets him choose a snack from her basket and he shows us all how he reads the label and enters his carbs. We cover a few more details before Denise says, "You're ready! You're going to love this once you get used to it." She shows him how he can clip the pump to his waistband or put it in his pocket and he chooses to clip it on. We are free to go.

That night at dinner I let him know how many carbs are on his plate and David watches over his shoulder while he enters the information into his pump. After dinner, we play some games and then David helps him disconnect the pump so he can take a shower. After he is reconnected, I crawl into bed with him, and he reads me a book. I kiss him goodnight and as I turn out the light, I say a prayer that he sleeps well and that the tubes aren't in his way.

At midnight, I check his blood sugar and notice he is a little high, so I enter his number in the pump and it automatically sends a correction of insulin. I'm back at three a.m. and when I check, he is low, so I wake him up and give him a juice box. Fifteen minutes later we retest, and his number is back in range. I'm grateful that he immediately falls back to sleep. I fill out the chart for Peds Endo and go back to bed, but I can't fall asleep. I'm thinking about the pump and the tubes and how they peek out from underneath his shirt. It's such a visible reminder of what we deal with daily. I'm wondering how his friends will react in school and hoping he won't be self-conscious. Different scenarios play out in my head, imaging how people may react. I pray for kindness and acceptance and finally I wear myself out and fall asleep.

Twenty-one

It's walk day and the weather is perfect. Sunny and seventy-five degrees makes for a beautiful day in the park. I fill a backpack with Sean's supplies and throw in some extra snacks and glucose tablets just in case. We put on the T-shirts Valerie dropped off that read "John's Posse" and drive to the park. Karen, Sherry and the boys are there already and just as we finish saying hello, Abby arrives with Noah. Sean introduces the boys while I introduce Abby to Karen and Sherry. We all make our way to the team tables and see the sign for "John's Posse." There is music playing, bouncy houses set up for the kids and inflatable slides on the grass. I notice Karen and Sherry are keeping a little distance from us but assume once we start walking, we will all be together. Looking around, I'm amazed by the turnout. Everywhere I look, I see little ones with wires sticking out of shirts and I am shocked by how many kids have T1D. I had no idea. I blink back the tears and try not to get too emotional as the realization that we are not alone sinks in.

My thoughts are interrupted by a woman holding a microphone and calling for everyone's attention. She introduces herself, makes some announcements, and then asks everyone to gather so we can begin our walk around the park. The boys come running back and we all huddle together as the crowd counts down from ten to one, and then everyone begins moving forward. Abby, Valerie, and I are walking with Sherry and Karen. David and Mike are walking ahead of us with the kids. Abby is telling us about a new restaurant she and her husband tried last week when I notice that slowly Sherry and Karen are separating themselves and walking ahead of us. They are deep in conversation and don't seem to realize or care that they have left us behind. Valerie and Abby seem to notice the shift; they look over at me and shrug. I shrug back.

I don't have too much time to think about it, because after they separate from us, Valerie says, "Mike made me so mad this morning. We were in the car ready to pull out of the driveway when he asked John if he remembered his bag of supplies. John looked at me, clearly hoping that I had it, while I surveyed the backseat and realized his backpack was missing. I told Mike he had to stop the car so I could run back into the house, and he got all high and mighty, moaning and groaning about how unorganized I am. Some days I just can't keep up." Abby and I glance at each other, not knowing how to respond, when Valerie changes the subject and lightens the mood.

We end up having a great time and once we get to the finish line, I feel like we are all old friends. When I look around for Sherry and Karen, I notice they are at the snack table, and after an internal debate about whether-or-not I should walk over to them, I decide against it. When it's time to leave, I hug Valerie and thank her for inviting us. Abby hugs us both and says she had a great time and appreciated being included. Karen and Sherry gather their boys and wave goodbye. Neither of them say goodbye to Valerie or Abby.

I am so embarrassed that my friends acted the way they did that I'm left wondering why they even came. I know I haven't been myself since Sean was diagnosed. I'm reminded of the "baby fog" era right after Sean was born, when nights and days were messed up, everything blurred together and the only focus was on my baby. Well, that's exactly how I feel now. Half the time I feel like a zombie. I haven't slept through the night since he was diagnosed. I'm forgetful and emotional and so badly want to go back to normal.

Twenty-two

I'm driving to work Monday morning, when Valerie calls. I thank her again for including us in the walk and apologize for the way Karen and Sherry behaved. She is more than gracious about it.

"Please don't think twice about it, Jessie. Some of my friendships changed after John was diagnosed and I've come to realize that some people are just uncomfortable with our 'new normal' and don't handle it well. Honestly, I have no bandwidth to think about them. It's all I can do to take care of John and Mike. It's truly their loss."

"I agree, Valerie. It's just sad to me that we were friends for so long and I know they care about us, but it has changed our friendship so much. I'm just glad I have you and Abby. You both understand and are so supportive. I hope I'm a support for you as well."

"You are! As a matter of fact, the reason I'm calling is to ask if you would be interested in joining the Breakthrough T1D gala committee? The gala is next spring and it's a great way to meet people. Our first meeting is in two weeks. Would you join me?"

"Yes, definitely. I'd love to help any way I can."

"Great. I will send you the information and we can drive to the meeting together. I'll plan on picking you up."

After we hang up, I feel so much better. I'm not sure what I'm getting myself into, but I've volunteered with non-profits before and know that it takes a village to put these events together. I do a little research and learn that Breakthrough T1D was founded by moms whose sons were diagnosed with T1D in the seventies. There wasn't a lot of research taking place and little was being done to advance treatments. Together, they began advocating to lawmakers for money for research and slowly a grassroots effort was underway to create a volunteer organization. Over the years the organization grew, and today they are international. I read up on their mission to advance treatments and ultimately cure T1D and decide I'm all in.

When David comes home, I follow him into our bedroom, and while he changes into sweatpants and a T-shirt I tell him what I learned about Breakthrough T1D and how excited I am to get involved. He is so encouraging, and the more I share with him, the more excited he becomes. Since Sean was diagnosed, David has been learning all he can about the research trials taking place, though I admit that most of what he explains to me goes over my head. But I really admire his talent for digesting the information and understanding what it means for Sean's future. When Sean was first diagnosed, we promised him we would do everything in our power to fight this disease and in this moment, I believe we have found a way to honor that promise.

The night before the gala meeting I barely get any sleep. Sean's blood sugar keeps dropping and I have to wake him multiple times to eat. The poor kid is chewing glucose tablets and drinking juice with his eyes closed, barely able to sit up. He finally stabilizes around four a.m. but by then I am so overtired I can't fall asleep, so I lie in bed with my eyes closed until the alarm goes off. I throw on sweatpants and a T-shirt, then wake Sean, who complains the entire time he gets ready, barely eats his breakfast and dozes off in the car on the way to school. I notice Noah walking into school just as I pull up, and, apparently Sean sees him too, because he perks up, jumps out of the car, and runs to catch up with him. As they walk in together, smiling and laughing, I breathe a sigh of relief, then go home and search my closet for something to wear to the meeting. Five outfit try-ons later, I settle on a pair of navy pants with a button-down blouse and cardigan.

Eleven-thirty on the dot, Valerie pulls in to my driveway, honking her horn. On our way to the Breakthrough T1D office, she fills me in on the volunteers who work on the gala. The committee consists of twelve men and women who are already gathered around the conference table when we arrive. As we take our seats, a woman whom I immediately recognize from the walk enters the room, greeting people by name as she sets her things on the table in front of her chair. She is about five-foot-two with blond hair, blue eyes and comes across as very warm and kind.

"Welcome, everyone. I really appreciate your taking time out of your day to join us to discuss our plans for the upcoming gala. We have a new volunteer joining us today." She turns to smile at me, and I return the smile as she continues, "Let's take a moment and go around the table to introduce ourselves. Please share your name and your connection to T1D. I will start. I'm Hope McGinnis. I joined Breakthrough T1D two years ago as development director and I love my job. While my aunt was my first connection to T1D, I like to think I have many connections after getting to know all of you and your families." She then turns to the woman on her right, and nods in her direction, indicating she should go next. I assumed the committee would be made up of moms, but I was wrong. There were adults with T1D, parents of T1D children, and even a forty-year-old man who was diagnosed with T1D just last year. No one flinches when someone's pump starts beeping, signaling an alert for low insulin levels, or someone else pulls out a meter to check their blood sugar.

As the discussion progresses, I find myself getting excited about joining this group and helping with the event. I'm motivated to raise money for a cure and hopeful I can help make a difference for Sean. Some of the volunteers take on leadership roles, including Valerie, who agrees to chair procurement for the auction. Two hours fly by and before I know it, we are in the car heading home. Valerie and I talk the whole way about the items she would like to get for the auction, and I agree to help her. I can't thank her enough for including me.

That night at dinner I don't stop talking. I'm telling David and Sean about the people I met, the event they are putting together and how excited I am to help Valerie. They both give me ideas for fun things to auction off and I write them down, so I don't forget.

Twenty-three

The next few months are busy with work, school activities, sports and gala meetings. I still check Sean's blood sugar throughout the night. Every Thursday, I fax over Sean's blood sugar log to Peds Endo and Denise calls me first thing Friday to make changes to his pump settings. This disease is so frustrating. Every time I think we have a good system, his numbers start to spike or drop and we have to make changes. Dr. Aronson assures us this is normal. He reminds us that with type 1 diabetes you can eat the same things every day, follow the same routine with the same amount of exercise daily, and your numbers will be completely different from one day to the next. Trying to regulate Sean's blood sugar is like playing whack-a-mole. Every time we hit one target, another one pops up.

It's finally gala weekend. Valerie and Mike have invited us to sit at their table and David and I are both looking forward to the evening. Our favorite babysitter, Kaitlyn, will stay with Sean. She's so sweet. When Sean was first diagnosed, we taught her how to check his blood sugar and what to do if he has a low. In the beginning, I never left him more than two hours. I was concerned that his blood sugar would be high, and I didn't feel comfortable asking her to give him shots. But now that he has the pump, it's much easier. He can adjust his insulin with the push of a button if he is running high. David and I have always reserved Saturday night for our "date night." Even if that meant a quick dinner and a trip to Walmart, it was our time alone. After Sean was diagnosed, I had to force myself to continue our Saturday night ritual, knowing how important it was to maintain as much normalcy as possible for Sean and for him to have confidence that he was ok. But it took a lot of hard work on my part to control my imagination and continue on as "normal." It's still nerve-racking for me to be away from Sean.

Friday afternoon I meet the committee at the venue to help set up the display for the auction items. Saturday, I have my hair styled, then rush home to put on my makeup and slip into a silky black gown. David is ready before me, and he looks exceptionally handsome in his tuxedo. I can't remember the last time we dressed up to go out. I'm making small talk with Kaitlyn when David nudges me, hinting that it's time to go, so I give Sean a quick kiss on the forehead and we head out the door.

When we arrive, the valet takes our car, and we walk through the lobby to the cocktail reception. Across the room, Valerie and Mike are talking with another couple, so David gets us drinks at the bar — gin and tonic for him, water for me — and we peruse the auction items.

We bid on a few things, including some sports memorabilia for Sean, and a Carolina Panthers family four-pack that includes tickets to an upcoming Panthers game and pre-game field passes. After an hour, an announcement is made inviting guests into the ballroom, so we find our table and introduce ourselves to Valerie's guests. Valerie and Mike join us just as my phone starts vibrating, and when I look down to see it's Kaitlyn calling, I excuse myself and answer.

"Is everything ok, Kaitlyn?"

"I'm not sure. We were playing and Sean's wire got caught on a toy and it looks like the needle is half in and half out. He says it hurts."

"I'm only ten minutes away. I'll be right home. See if you can get him to pull it off. If not, just sit still. I'm on my way."

Adrenaline is racing through me as I tell David what happened, holding out my hand impatiently as he fishes through his pocket for the valet ticket. He wants to come with me, but I encourage him to stay with Valerie and Mike and quickly leave the ballroom. The second the valet brings our car around, I jump inside and drive home, gripping the steering wheel so tightly that my knuckles are white.

I pull into the driveway and run straight into the house to find Sean and Kaitlyn sitting on the couch. He was too afraid to touch the needle so it's still dangling. I quickly remove it, and he starts bleeding, so I grab some tissues and press it against his stomach. While I wait for the bleeding to stop, I make conversation by asking questions about what they were playing and if they picked out a movie for later. Outwardly, I'm so calm you would think this happened every day. The truth is, I'm a mess inside. I swear if they gave out Oscars to moms who have to act like everything is ok when it clearly isn't, I would win hands down. Once the bleeding stops, I get out a new reservoir, fill it with insulin and prime the pump. We place the needle on the opposite side of his stomach, and I sit with him a few minutes to make sure he is ok. Then I have him test and he is a little high, so he has the pump release insulin and I remind Kaitlyn to test him again in two hours and text me his blood sugar number. I don't want to leave but realize once again I have to show him that diabetes can't stop us, so I kiss him goodbye and head out the door.

I arrive back at our table just as they are serving the main course. Valerie stands and hugs me, and David squeezes my hand as I sit down beside him. After dinner the live auction begins. There are bidding wars over several items and it's fun to watch people compete for these packages. Following the auction, the emcee introduces the keynote speaker, whose son has type 1 diabetes. Once he shares his diagnosis story and his worries for his son, there isn't a dry eye in the house, including my own. Seriously, how many tears can one body manufacture? You would think mine were depleted by now, but I seem to have an endless supply. After sharing his story, the speaker appeals to the audience to please donate generously, reminding us all that, "Breakthrough T1D is our hope to cure type 1 diabetes." When the auctioneer returns to the stage, he instructs everyone to locate their bid cards and asks the crowd if anyone is willing to donate $50,000 and my mouth drops open and I nudge David when I see a bid card raised, followed by another one. Once he is satisfied that all the bids at that level are acknowledged, he moves to a $25,000 level and again a few bid cards are raised. This continues in lower increments until everyone in the room has participated, including us. David proudly raised his card, surprising me at the $1000 level. Valerie leans over and hugs him. The generosity in the room is beyond belief and the crowd goes wild when they announce the grand total raised. WOW! What a night.

On the ride home David and I talk nonstop about how inspired we are and how motivated we feel to get more involved. I want to meet other families living with T1D and raise as much money as we can to cure this awful disease. For the first time since Sean was diagnosed, I feel as if I can do something about it. Until now I couldn't see a way out but now, I do. I'm determined that we can make a difference in Sean's future.

Twenty-four

A few days after the gala I get a call from Hope. She says she would like to get to know me and invites me to lunch at a café near her office. I mention it to Valerie, and she is encouraging. When I arrive at the café, Hope is already seated, and she smiles as I slide into the booth across from her and thank her for the invitation. We chat about the gala, how generous the community is, and she tells me more about her job. After the waitress takes our order, Hope asks if I would be interested in working on the walk committee for next year. The gala and walk are their two big fundraisers, with the gala taking place in the spring and the walk in the fall.

"Committee work is a great way to bond with other T1D families and we could really use your help." When I agree to volunteer, Hope gives me an overview of the different roles on the committee and suggests I attend a few meetings before deciding what role I want to take on.

As I'm leaving lunch the school nurse calls. She says Sean's blood sugar is unusually high and he doesn't feel well. She's been giving him insulin through the pump, but it doesn't seem to be working. I rush over to the school and pick him up. He looks pale, complains of nausea and is holding his stomach. I feel his forehead but it's cool, so we rush home and check his blood sugar again. The meter displays the word HIGH which indicates his number is over 400 so I give him a shot and we change his pump site. I glance at the clock and make a mental note of the time and then I set him up on the couch with a pillow and blanket. He dozes off as I step into the kitchen to grab something to drink when my phone rings. I check Caller ID and see its Abby.

"Hi Jessie. How is Sean? Noah said he had to leave school early because he wasn't feeling well."

I tell her what happened, and she immediately asks what she can do to help and even offers to come sit with me if I want company until he feels better. I tell her how much that means to me, but really, I think he will be fine once his blood sugar is back in range. We catch up on some school gossip and as soon as we hang up, anther call comes through, this time from the rabbi.

It's been a while since she called and when I answer the phone, I immediately wish I had sent it to voicemail. She's calling because we haven't been to Friday night services in a long time, and she wants to know what's going on. I start making excuses and then stop myself and tell her the truth, which is that it's not where I want to be right now. I am so angry at God that when I think about sitting in synagogue, saying the same prayers I've said over and over through the years, it leaves me feeling empty.

She surprises me by trying to argue that God is helping us through this by giving us strength and that if we come to services, we may find some comfort in our community. I argue back that if there is a God, why would this happen? There is no way we are going to see eye-to-eye on this right now, and while I would like to agree to disagree, she becomes more persistent until finally I cut her off and tell her that Sean needs me, hanging up just as my alarm reminds me to recheck his blood sugar. He is still asleep, so I gently stick his finger and am relieved to see 150 pop up on the screen. I kiss his forehead and leave him to sleep.

Twenty-five

It's hard to believe it's been a whole year since Sean was diagnosed. This summer will look a lot different than last summer. For one, Sean decided he didn't want to go back to camp. Noah and John are both attending a variety of week-long summer programs and Sean would like to be with them. He chooses a film-making camp with John and a Lego robotics camp with Noah. I've worked out a carpool plan with both Abby and Valerie and I'm looking forward to the break from sitting in car lines. Surprisingly, I receive a random call from Sherry at the end of June. We haven't spoken since religious school let out over a month ago, so we briefly catch up but neither one of us initiates getting together.

Work is so busy. All the college graduates are looking for jobs and we are overloaded with resumés. Helen and I meet on Monday mornings to review the candidates and match them with potential opportunities and then I get to work setting up their profiles and arranging their interviews. On my two days off a week, I spend my time attending meetings for the walk and really enjoy the committee work. The new friends I'm making invigorate me, and I find it comforting to be around people who understand T1D. If someone walks into the meeting and says they are tired from chasing a high blood sugar all night, we all get it.

My role on the committee is community awareness and publicity, so I spend time with Hope brainstorming our marketing strategy. David is a huge help to me, as I continuously pick his brain for ideas on how to best market the event and the organization locally. With his guidance, I reach out to all the local TV stations and am pleasantly surprised with the response. I'm able to schedule several interviews for Hope and our walk chairperson Marcy, who was diagnosed as a child and is very comfortable sharing her story. Channel 4's evening news producer sends a camera crew to Marcy's house to film her testing her blood sugar and giving herself insulin shots, which they will show during their live TV interview. When I reach out to the producer of a local morning talk show, he agrees to dedicate an entire segment to the walk.

The walk kick-off luncheon has been scheduled a month prior to the event and team leaders, along with current and potential walk sponsors, VIP donors and committee members are all invited. A few weeks before the luncheon, Valerie and I are at the office stuffing walk packets when Hope asks to see me. After I follow her into her office and sit down in the chair facing her desk, I'm caught completely off-guard when she leans forward with her elbows on the desk and asks me to be the keynote speaker at the luncheon.

I stare at her in disbelief. "Me?"

"Yes, you! You have a great story to share."

"What would I talk about?"

"You could share Sean's story, what led to his diagnosis, how you came to volunteer with Breakthrough T1D and what it has meant to you. It's only a little over a year since your son was diagnosed and you've already volunteered on the gala and now the walk. I think you could inspire a lot of people. What do you say? Please?"

I sit back thinking about what my message would be. Could I really inspire someone else to get more involved?

I'm not a fan of public speaking so I surprise myself by saying, "Yes, I'll do it."

Hope jumps up and comes around the desk to hug me. "Thank you so much! I'm happy to help proofread once you write your speech."

"Thanks! Can you deliver it, too?" We share a laugh before I tell her, "I'm happy to help any way I can."

Twenty-six

The day of the luncheon, Valerie picks me up so we can go together. We meet up with David and Mike in the lobby and I can't help but notice that Valerie and Mike barely acknowledge each other. Mike is completely engaged in a conversation with David which makes me feel a little uncomfortable when I interrupt them so I can introduce David to a few of the committee members. At the table, David and I claim our seats and Valerie immediately sits down beside me, so naturally I expect Mike to sit down next to Valerie, but instead he sits next to David. When I ask Valerie if everything is ok, she shrugs and looks away.

After Hope is satisfied that everyone has had a chance to eat and socialize, she approaches the microphone, welcomes everyone, and acknowledges some key people. My heart starts to race a little and my palms feel sweaty as she begins to introduce me. I take out my notes, blot my lips with my napkin and whisper to David, "Here I go."

He whispers in my ear, "You've got this. You're a rock star."

I squeeze his hand and turn my attention back to Hope, just in time to hear her share a little about me and my background.

"Friends, please join me in welcoming our keynote speaker, Jessie Greene."

I approach the stage and thank Hope for the introduction. The next three minutes feel like an out-of-body experience. Briefly, I share our story, express how life-changing it was for me when I met Valerie, and when she introduced me to Hope and Breakthrough T1D. I implore everyone to get involved and to raise as much money as possible, and before I know it, people are applauding, and Hope is giving me a hug. When I return to our table David is standing with a big grin. "You knocked it out of the ballpark." I hug him and take my seat. I'm a little overwhelmed and greatly surprised when other guests approach me after the program to thank me for sharing my story. I immediately recognize the moms whose kids were recently diagnosed by the tears in their eyes and the look of shock on their faces. Exchanging phone numbers with a few of them, I encourage them to reach out for support. Out of the corner of my eye I notice Mike say good-bye to David and slip out the door while Valerie stays seated at the table.

On the ride home, Valerie is unusually quiet, so when we reach my house, I turn to face her, place my hand on her shoulder and ask her what's wrong. Her floodgates open and tears are rolling down her face as she tells me that she and Mike had an argument the night before that carried over to this morning, all because she wanted to explore middle school options for John. She's not happy about the school they are zoned for, but Mike thinks she is over-controlling and should just leave it alone, even though she is concerned about John because the school doesn't have the best reputation. I suggest she tour the school Sean will attend, which has a magnet program for the arts, something that is a big interest for John. I also mention that the best part is that once you're in the program, it feeds into the same high school that Sean and Noah will attend. Valerie perks up when I give her the number for the main office.

Twenty-seven

This year we formed our own walk team, "Sean's Brigade." Sean invited some school friends along, including Noah, and David had T-shirts made for everyone. Sean also insisted on inviting Billy and Cory, who he still sees on Sunday mornings, now that school is back in session. I was pleasantly surprised when they accepted the invitation.

The backseat of my car is loaded down with T-shirts as I drive from house to house delivering them to everyone on our walk team. When I get to Karen's house, she invites me into the kitchen, where she makes us some coffee and takes out a tin of homemade cookies. Making small talk, I happen to glance over toward the counter, where my eyes land on a picture of Karen and Sherry with their families. They are all wearing the Mickey ears you get at Disney World. I see the Dumbo ride in the background and realize they must have gone away together. Her eyes follow mine toward the picture and then back to me. "We went over the summer."

Before I can stop myself, I say, "Wow. Wish we had been included in that trip. Looks like fun."

"Yeah, it was. We didn't think you would want to go

away. You know, with Sean."

"Karen, what's going on? Do you really think we can't travel because of Sean, or is there something else happening here? Is it something I did?"

"No, you didn't do anything. We just figured Sean's condition would make it challenging for you to get around the park."

Anger boils up inside of me and it's all I can do to stop myself from screaming. In a controlled, clipped tone I say, "While it hurts to be left out, you and Sherry are entitled to do things without me. I'm not sure how or why our friendship changed, and I certainly don't want you to feel obligated to include me if you prefer not to. But don't you dare blame it on Sean. He can do anything he wants to do. Diabetes will not slow him down nor will it stop him. I won't allow it." I give her a long look, willing my eyes not to brim, and then I grab my bag and walk out the door.

On walk day we get to the park early, find our table with the "Sean's Brigade" sign above it and set out some snacks. Much to my surprise, there is no sign of Karen when Sherry shows up with Cory and Billy. She is friendly but keeps her distance, giving me a clear signal that Karen told her what happened between us and, obviously, she doesn't want to discuss it. Sherry is typically kindhearted and very easily swayed, so I'm convinced she wants to stay out of whatever is going on between me and Karen. Unfortunately, it has now driven a wedge between me and Sherry. Still, I am grateful she came and brought the boys. It would have been disappointing to Sean if they weren't here. At one point I walk over to try to make conversation, but it is awkward, so I excuse myself to use the restroom before we start walking. Later, Valerie tells me that when she and Abby recognized Sherry, they attempted to talk to her and, although Sherry was cordial, she didn't overextend herself and they gave up.

We agree with the kids that if we get separated during the walk we will meet back at our team table. Sherry spots a friend from Billy's school and walks with her. After making our way through the course, we are back at our table when I spot the boys coming off the trail and watch with amusement as Sean and John break away from their group and come running over.

"Guess what?" they both yell at the same time.

"What?" I say, trying to match their enthusiasm.

"There's a dunk tank and Dr. Aronson is in it! Can we have money to play? We know we can dunk him!" I laugh as I give them each five dollars. I look over and notice how long the line is. I guess a lot of people want to dunk Dr. Aronson.

Twenty-eight

We are in desperate need of a family vacation, so we decide to drive to Florida over winter break. Abby and Valerie both want to join us, so Abby invites us all to her house for a group dinner and planning session, where we all meet Abby's husband Frank, who is as warm and welcoming as Abby is. Abby could be a travel agent; she is so good at vacation planning! She finds us the perfect house to rent on the beach and scouts out activities to keep us busy.

Valerie and I commiserate with each other over needing an extra suitcase for a week's worth of diabetes supplies, but it doesn't dampen our excitement. The trip turns out to be my favorite get-away to date. Everyone gets along, Valerie and Mike seem to be in a good place and diabetes even behaves itself, except for a few daytime lows from too much fun in the ocean.

On our last night together, sitting around the back deck of the rental, Mike asks Frank and David if they would want to plan a guys' weekend with the boys. He suggests an overnight trip to Atlanta to see a Hawks basketball game. The boys hear Mike and immediately start to chant "Hawks, Hawks, Hawks!" as they slap their hands on the table.

Abby turns to me and Valerie with a huge grin. "Ladies, I see a mom's night out for us!"

"Absolutely, I'm in!" Valerie says as we clink our wine glasses together.

Later that night, I find myself smiling while I pack our suitcases.

"What's that grin about?" David asks as he hands me Sean's bathing suit.

"I was just thinking about how happy I feel. This trip was amazing." I lean over to kiss him, and he pulls me in for a hug.

Twenty-nine

Back home, Valerie and I meet for our weekly coffee and catch-up. She is beaming as she tells me that Mike finally caved, and they have an appointment with the Morris Middle School. I'm so excited! Immediately I envision us joining the Parent Organization together and the boys getting involved in various school activities.

The next day I'm at work on pins and needles, anxiously watching my phone, when finally, Valerie calls. It's immediately clear to me that she and Mike took separate cars to Morris Middle, because the minute I answer the phone, the first words out of her mouth are, "Even grumpy Mike loves everything about the school." She goes on to tell me they were so impressed with the curriculum and activities that they filled out the application right on the spot. She can't wait to go back to pick up John, who is spending the afternoon shadowing a sixth grader. According to the principal, they should know within a few weeks if John has a spot for next year.

Two weeks later Valerie calls to tell me it's official. John will be attending school with Noah and Sean next year!

I go to bed so excited that night. I'm happy the boys

will go through school together and feel a sense of comfort that John and Sean can lean on each other as they face the challenge of navigating middle school and high school with diabetes.

It's two a.m. when I hear a loud, piercing noise coming from Sean's room. Awakened from a deep sleep, it takes me a minute to get my bearings. I run down the hall, grabbing a bottle of juice just in case he is going low. When I get to his room Sean is sitting up in bed, crying. The pump continues to make a horrible noise, and so I push the button on the screen to see if there is a message. It doesn't give me any indication of what is wrong, so I disconnect the tube and take the pump into the kitchen. I still can't get it to stop screaming at me. By now, David has joined the party and has calmed Sean down. He watches Sean test his blood sugar and then convinces him to lie down and rest while they wait for me to figure out what is happening. I call the toll-free number for the 24-hour help line and receive a message that I am number twenty-five in the queue, and they will be with me shortly.

After thirty minutes, I finally connect with a customer service person, who asks me a million questions, has me push several buttons on the pump and read him numbers, and then informs me the pump has failed. He gives me instructions on how to silence the alarm. They will overnight a new one to us, but since it won't go out until morning, we won't have it until the following day. Until then, we are back on shots.

When I go back into Sean's room, he is leaning against David with his eyes closed. I have to wake him to remove the needle still in his stomach. Since he just tested his blood sugar and it was in a good range, I don't have to give him a shot, so I tuck him in and tell him he is on a pump break until we get the new one. It's three-thirty in the morning by the time I crawl back into bed, and I spend the rest of the night staring at the ceiling, listening to David snore. I finally get out of bed at five-thirty, brew a pot of coffee and carry my mug onto the back deck to watch the sunrise. After nights like last night, I feel an increased sense of anxiety. I try to imagine Sean as an adult navigating this disease. How can one person manage all this by themselves? It's never-ending and I worry about the long-term impact his diabetes will have on him.

I'm practically jumping up and down for joy when the pump arrives two days later. When I call the help line, they guide me through the process as I transfer all the information from the recently deceased pump. And while we prime the new pump, we chant, "Hook Me Up, Hook, Hook Me Up." David and Sean pump their fists in the air, and I insert the needle.

"Superpowers have been restored!" I declare, and laugh as Sean pulls on his shirt.

Thirty

The guys are leaving Saturday for their basketball weekend in Atlanta, and Valerie, Abby and I are going for dinner and a movie. I'm working on my list of things to pack for Sean when the phone rings. It's Sherry calling to touch base and see if we want to get together Sunday after religious school. It's been a while since we've done that. We are all friendly when we see each other, but I stopped initiating, and they stopped calling.

"Thanks so much for calling, Sherry. Sean won't be in school on Sunday, so this week won't work for us."

"Is everything ok?" She knows it's not like us to miss school.

"Yes, everything is great. David and Sean have plans with friends for a guys' weekend away. I really appreciate the invitation. Maybe another time."

Saturday morning everyone meets at our house. Handing David a container of homemade muffins and some snacks I packed for the ride, I'm giggling at the boys as they climb into Mike's van. There's a lot of male energy heading toward Atlanta. I wave as they pull out of the driveway and step back into a very quiet house, not quite sure what to do with myself. Abby and Valerie are picking me up at five-thirty so I have all day to myself. I make myself a cup of tea, grab a book I've been wanting to read, and curl up under my favorite blanket on the couch. Within minutes my eyes are heavy, and I find myself fighting to concentrate so I place the book on the coffee table next to my still steaming cup of tea and close my eyes.

When I awake, I glance at the clock and notice it's three o'clock. I slept for four hours. I don't think I've slept four hours straight since Sean was diagnosed. I close my eyes again and another hour passes before I force myself to get up and make my way into the bathroom to start the shower. I take my time getting ready and then pour myself a glass of wine while I wait for Abby and Valerie to pick me up. Abby is our designated driver tonight. I haven't had a girl's night out since Nashville, but this time there is no apprehension.

When I hear Abby's horn beep, I grab my purse, lock up the house and find myself practically skipping as I approach the car.

"Ladies, are we ready for a fun night?" I ask as I close the car door.

Valerie smiles at me over her shoulder and says, "Absolutely! What did you do all day?"

"I slept! Literally all afternoon!"

"Me too." Valerie says.

"Not me," Abby gloats. "I splurged and treated myself to a luxurious massage, followed by a mani-pedi."

"You win!" Valerie and I say at the same time!

After a scrumptious dinner at a new Mexican restaurant, we go to the movies to see the latest rom-com, and by the time I get home my stomach muscles ache from all the laughing. David calls just as I am walking in the door, providing me with a play-by-play of their day. After we hang up, I climb into bed and turn on the TV, but within minutes I fall asleep. Startled, I jolt awake in the middle of the night, automatically jumping out of bed to go check on Sean, and then laugh at myself. I'm so used to waking up in the middle of the night it's almost impossible to sleep straight through. Once I climb back into bed, though, I fall into a deep sleep, and when I finally wake up, I stretch, reach for my phone and there's a message from David letting me know they were stopping for breakfast and then would be on their way home.

The Middle
School Years

Thirty-one

Time passes quickly and before I know it, Sean is entering middle school. I join the Parent Organization and volunteer in the bookstore weekly, giving me the opportunity to observe Sean with his friends. It warms my heart to watch him engage with them as they stand around laughing between classes. Between work, volunteering at the school and my committee work with Breakthrough T1D, I'm super busy. I've agreed to mentor newly diagnosed families and can't wait for my training session so I can get started. David worries that I am taking on too much, but I assure him I'm fine.

It's a Thursday night in November when David comes home and says he needs to talk with me. He's concerned that, aside from bringing Sean to religious school, we don't really attend synagogue as often as we used to. I'm caught a little off-guard and sit quietly while he expresses his desire to attend services more frequently. I'm still so conflicted over my feelings about God that I'm questioning the purpose of sitting through services, repeating prayers that have become meaningless for me. When I share this with him, his response surprises me.

He understands how I feel, but at the same time, this is important to him, and he wants me to support him by attending services, so I agree to go with him and Sean Friday night.

I'm extremely apprehensive as we enter the synagogue. The usual Friday night crowd is there, and I see Karen and Sherry already sitting in the pew we all used to share. As we enter the sanctuary, I take hold of David's arm and guide him toward the other side of the room. I notice Karen whisper something to Sherry and immediately, Sherry looks over her shoulder toward me, smiles and waves. I wave back and then focus my attention on Sean and David. I follow along with the service, willing myself to find some meaning or comfort in the words I've repeated since my childhood, but it evades me. Immediately following the service, Sean jumps out of his seat and runs over to Billy and Cory, and together they race to the dessert table. I hold onto David's hand as we enter the social hall and stand silently while he makes small talk, watching Sherry and Karen huddled in the corner chatting. As soon as there is a break in his conversation, I convince David we should leave and call for Sean to say good-bye to his friends. Staring out the window on the drive home, I listen to Sean and David happily chatting and I wonder what's wrong with me that I no longer feel any connection to a community I have invested so much of my time and energy in over the past ten years.

A few days later, Hope calls to ask if I would mentor a mom whose daughter was just diagnosed last week with T1D. Lisa is a single mom of two who desperately needs another parent to talk to, so I call her immediately, and arrange to meet her for coffee the following day. I've arrived at the coffee shop early to scout out a table in the back corner, so we'll have privacy, and when a woman enters, I recognize her immediately by the red-rimmed eyes and deer-in-the-headlights look on her face. After waving her over, I go to the counter to place our order, and once back at the table, I sit down, place my hand over her trembling hand, and ask, "How are you doing?"

Her eyes fill with tears as she answers, "Not great. I'm anxious all the time. I'm so afraid I'll do something wrong." I nod and tell her I know exactly how she feels. We talk for two hours and when we get up to leave, she hugs me and asks if we can meet again. "Yes, absolutely. Call me if you need anything. I'm here for you." I also invite her to bring her girls to the next walk, silently acknowledging the full circle moment with a flash-back to my first coffee with Valerie.

As confident as I felt talking to Lisa, there are still situations that stop me in my tracks. Just last night during my three a.m. blood sugar check, I thought I smelled insulin. I shone my little flashlight under the covers and felt around on the bed, but it was dry. When I lightly touched Sean's stomach, his nightshirt was wet; somehow the tube had dislodged and now his number was over 400. I woke him up and gave him a shot, handed him a clean shirt to change into and got everything ready so I could change his pump site. Sean couldn't keep his eyes open, so I had him lie on his back as I adhered the needle to his stomach while he slept, after which I spent the next hour on the couch, waiting to recheck his blood sugar. In the morning, Sean barely remembered the middle of the night site change, but I could barely function.

Thirty-two

At the start of seventh grade, Sean tries out for the middle school's basketball team. He makes the team and couldn't be more excited. We celebrate that night with a special dinner, and while he and David talk about the intricacies of the game, I'm thinking about how we are going to prevent low blood sugars. Practice is ninety minutes every day after school, a far cry from the weekly one-hour practice he attended for rec basketball. Do I talk to the coach? No middle schooler wants their mom talking to the coach. I'm at a loss, so I call Denise and ask for guidance. She suggests we talk when we come in for our quarterly visit next week.

The following Wednesday, I pick Sean up at lunch time for his appointment. The timing is good, since his practices will start after school on Monday. Dr. Aronson and Denise talk to Sean about how to "attempt" to manage his blood sugar during practices and games. They encourage him to have a snack before practice that includes protein, fat and carbs. We decide he will bring a bagel with peanut butter to school to eat before practice and then sip on Gatorade throughout practice. Because his pump has wires attached, they agree that he should disconnect from the pump during practice. This will leave him without insulin for around an hour to an hour and a half, and should help prevent a post-exercise low. After all this, Dr. Aronson tells us there is another pump on the market that he would like us to consider. It is a tubeless pod with a built-in reservoir that adheres to the stomach and can be worn for two to three days. The minute Sean hears there is a pump without wires he begs us to switch, prompting Denise to offer to contact our insurance company to make sure it's covered.

The next day Sean goes directly from his last class to practice. I'm sitting in the parking lot an hour prior to pick-up just in case there is an issue, reading a book to pass the time, and I'm so engrossed in the story that it startles me when I look up to see Sean coming out of the athletic center. As soon as he gets in the car, he tests his blood sugar, and his number is actually high because he forgot to put in the carbs for the bagel before disconnecting the pump. He enters a correction dose and two hours later his blood sugar drops, and he is low. We repeat the pattern for a few days and then, out of nowhere, during practice one day he goes low. Twice. I'm still sitting in the parking lot during practice so when the coach's assistant calls to say they are having trouble stabilizing Sean's blood sugar, I run into the building and give him more glucose tablets with a snack. By the time his number is in a good range, practice is over. The next morning, I call Denise and tell her our plan isn't working. She offers a few suggestions and reminds me this is all trial and error until we find what works for Sean.

Friday night is the home opening game so there is no practice. Sean has to report to the school gym an hour before game time, so David and I drop him off, then park the car. We had loaded Sean's gym bag with extra glucose tablets, two bottles of Gatorade and a snack to eat before the game starts. I hope he remembers to bring it to the bench.

After David and I find seats halfway up on the bleachers, we chat with the other parents while we wait for the game to start. Out of the corner of my eye I watch as the team comes out of the locker room and starts to warm up, breathing a sigh of relief when I see Sean carry his bag and place it on the bench. As I watch him practice his layups, for a brief moment, I pretend he doesn't have diabetes, and just take pride in how athletic he is. When the whistle blows and the teams return to the bench, I realize I'm holding my breath. Attempting to calm my nerves, I begin counting backwards from ten, trying to focus on my breathing, when I notice Sean is in the starting lineup.

As the game progresses, I feel as if I'm having an out-of-body experience. Sitting on the edge of my seat on the bleachers and carefully watching Sean for any sign that he is not feeling well, I glance around and notice the other parents who are watching their kids running back and forth across the court. I've never been a jealous person, but I envy them now as they mindlessly cheer for their kids. To an outside observer, I probably look just like them. Smiling, leaning forward, cheering when someone makes a basket. But inside, I'm holding my breath and preparing myself for anything that could go wrong. I'm praying that his blood sugar doesn't drop. That he remembers to drink some Gatorade when he's back on the bench. That the coach is paying attention to him and recognizes when he may need to take a break and has the smarts to send in a sub so Sean can rest. It takes all my self-control to not embarrass him by running to the bench at half-time to remind him to check his blood sugar.

It's too much. I feel that old anger bubbling up again. I'm just plain angry at life, at God and even at diabetes for taking away my son's carefree childhood. And I juggle all these emotions while outwardly smiling and pretending I'm ok. Because what choice do I have? I know Sean will take his cues from David and me and I want him to feel confident and secure. I don't want him to be defined by diabetes. I'm trying to set a good example for my son. So, I smile, act like I know what I'm doing and tell myself that everything is going to be ok.

Thirty-three

We finally get the call from Denise that the new tubeless pump has been approved. She offers us a date to attend a training session, and I confirm we are available and will be there. It means pulling Sean out of school again, but it's worth it. When the day comes, David, Sean and I pile into the Peds Endo training room. I'm convinced I have PTSD from our first morning here after Sean was diagnosed, since the minute we step into the room I feel clammy. Denise offers us water and then she gets started transferring his settings from the old pump to the new controller, explaining every step along the way. It takes a while because the screen prompts are different, but we finally get everything entered. When it comes time to fill the insulin reservoir, Denise offers the syringe and insulin to Sean. He shakes his head no, so she passes it across the table to me. I fill the pod and adhere it to Sean's stomach. There is a button to push on the controller and that inserts the cannula under his skin. After we count down "three, two, one," I push the button, causing Sean to flinch a little before he rubs the adhesive around the pod. Denise offers him a snack and watches him enter his carbs into the controller. Unlike the first pump, which was attached by the tubing, this pump has a separate controller, which Sean will have to carry with him at all times. While I gather our supplies, David takes Sean to check out at the front desk.

"Jessie," Denise begins, standing to help me. "Sean is doing a great job. He seems very well adjusted."

"Thanks Denise. I just wish he would fill the reservoir or try to put the pump on himself. He manages everything else, but this seems harder for him."

"He'll do it in his own time, Jessie. He has a long road ahead. Think of it as a marathon, not a race, and let him pace himself. I promise he'll do it on his own when he's ready. You and David are doing a great job with him."

I thank her for the encouragement, and hurry to catch up with David and Sean.

When we get home, I call Valerie. John is considering a switch to the wireless pump, so they come over for Sean to show it to him. While the boys run off to play, Valerie and I get a drink and sit on the deck. It's a little chilly, so we grab blankets to cover our legs. Valerie is venting about an old friend she ran into at the grocery store, who asked Valerie how John was managing with his diabetes. When Valerie responded that he was doing great, the well-meaning but misinformed friend suggested, "You know, if you would give John coconut oil, it would cure his diabetes." Valerie thanked her for the information and excused herself from the conversation. She follows that up by telling me that when John was first diagnosed, an elderly relative told her that taking him to a chiropractor would cure him. We share a good laugh over that one and, knowing Mike is away overnight on a business trip, I invite Valerie and John to stay for dinner. She agrees to stay, so I tell her to rest on the deck while I go inside to prepare dinner. But when I happen to glance out the window as I'm cooking, I see her wipe away a few tears. I wash off my hands and go back outside.

"Valerie, are you ok?"

She takes a tissue from her pocket and wipes her eyes.

"What's wrong?" I ask again.

"Sometimes I'm just so sad, and I can't even talk to Mike about it because he minimizes what I'm feeling and tells me I overthink everything. After all this time, I still worry about John and how he's going to manage this all on his own. What happens when they go to college?"

"We'll go with them," I say, with a chuckle that makes her smile. "Valerie, it is overwhelming and of course you're going to worry about him. When he's married with children you will still worry about him. I met a woman last week at a gala meeting who is fifty years old. Her mother still calls her every morning to ask her what her blood sugar is. We're moms...that's what we do."

I lean in and hug her. "They're going to be ok because we're going to be ok. We're going to teach them how to take care of themselves and we're going to be there to support them. And we have each other."

I step back into the kitchen and finish making dinner. As I do so, I silently say a little prayer to the God I don't know if I believe in anymore. *Please dear God, watch over our boys. Keep them safe and healthy.* Then I say a little thank you for Valerie.

Thirty-four

In the midst of all the middle-school activities and basketball games, Sean has been practicing for his bar mitzvah, a rite of passage for a thirteen-year-old boy in the Jewish faith. He has learned to read from the Torah and will lead Saturday morning services. Our families are flying in from across the country. David and I have gone all out on the party planning. We will be hosting a dinner Friday night for our families and have arranged for a luncheon at the synagogue after Saturday morning services. Saturday night will be the big celebration with all our friends and family at a local catering hall. In total, we are expecting 150 guests for Saturday night. For the past year, David, Sean and I have brainstormed ideas, talked about themes, menus and decorations.

This is also the year that Cory and Billy will celebrate their bar mitzvahs. Cory's party is first and is being held at a local hotel. We have an understanding at the synagogue that all the kids in the bar mitzvah class are invited to each other's celebrations, so I'm not surprised when the invitation arrives in the mail. What does surprise me is seeing that David and I are included on the invitation.

I still see Karen and Sherry at synagogue, and we are always cordial, but since that afternoon in Karen's house when I discovered they went to Disney World without us, we don't really talk much. She never apologized, and I moved on. Sherry had made it crystal clear her loyalty was to Karen, and so The Three Musketeers broke up. Seeing the invitation makes me nostalgic, though, so impulsively, I pick up the phone and dial her number. She doesn't answer so I leave a message to thank her, congratulate the family, and say that we look forward to celebrating with them. I hang up and wipe a little tear from my eye. I wish we could go back in time before everything became insurmountable. I miss my friends.

At dinner that night, I show David and Sean Cory's invitation. Sean tells us the boys were talking about their parties at Sunday school. Apparently, Billy is having a soccer-themed party, and since Cory wants to be an astronaut, he is having an outer space theme. Sean had decided on a football theme, so we are decorating in black, white and blue in honor of his favorite team, the Carolina Panthers.

The next day at our check-up with Dr. Aronson he introduces us to a CGM — a continuous glucose monitor. He takes a new one out of its packaging and shows us how it works, explaining that the hair-thin sensor is inserted under the skin using an applicator, and then a transmitter clips on top of the adhesive between little plastic brackets. The sensor can read blood sugar levels every five minutes and sends the information through the transmitter to a handheld receiver.

"Not only will it tell you what your blood sugar level is, but it tells you where it is going with arrows. If the arrow points straight it means you are steady, and if it points up or down it means you are going high or low. You enter your preferred range in the receiver, and it will alarm you if your number goes over or below that range."

He suggests that we put one on Sean and try it for a week. A sensor can be worn for seven days before it needs to be removed and replaced with a new one. At first, Sean is hesitant. He wants to know if it hurts. Dr. Aronson says it's a little pinch, just like when he inserts the pod. He wants to know where he would wear it, and Dr. Aronson says he can wear it on his stomach opposite the pod or he can wear it on the back of his arm. Sean is chewing on his bottom lip, thinking it through, when Dr. Aronson says, "You know, if you are wearing this you won't have to stick your finger as much to test your blood sugar. You can just look at the receiver to check it." Then he looks at me and says "With the alarm system, you won't have to wake up in the middle of the night anymore. The CGM will alarm you if Sean's blood sugar is out of range."

I look at Sean, who still seems nervous. "Hey, Sean."

He looks up at me and I smile at him. He reluctantly agrees. "Let's try it."

"Great idea," I say.

I can't help but marvel at how far Sean has come and how brave he is. Before he was diagnosed, if he needed any kind of shot, we had to chase him around the office or hold him down as he kicked and screamed. He still looks scared, but he takes a deep breath and braces himself when Denise walks us through each step as she puts the CGM on Sean's stomach. Apparently, it hurts a little more than the pod, but he sits still and rubs the adhesive, and in a minute, he is back to himself.

The week goes smoothly. The alarm goes off a few times, mostly for low blood sugars, and one night for a high blood sugar after a pizza dinner. Pizza is the worst because all the fat slows down the absorption of the insulin, so it can take hours after eating to come down. It did alarm in school one day after lunch, but Sean didn't mind because it got him out of "a boring science class." When we return to the office for Denise to remove the sensor, we tell her we want to move forward and have Sean wear the CGM. Denise was so confident we would like it, she had already checked our insurance coverage and arranged for the company that makes the CGM to mail us a three-month supply.

Thirty-five

I'm engrossed in a project at work when my phone rings, and although I don't recognize the number, I answer anyway, hoping it's the rep from the CGM company.

"Mrs. Greene? This is Charlotte, the nurse at Piper Middle School. You are listed as the emergency contact for Cory Springer. I can't reach Mrs. Springer and Cory is running a fever and needs to be picked up."

"Are you sure I'm the one listed as an emergency backup and not Sherry Landers?"

"Sherry is listed as the first contact, and you are her back-up. I couldn't reach her either. I tried Mr. Springer, but his secretary said he is in a meeting and can't be disturbed. Can you please pick up Cory?"

"I'll be right there." I hang up and try calling Karen. It goes right to voicemail. I leave her a message and tell her I am picking Cory up and will bring him to her house. I call Sherry's phone and when she doesn't answer, I just hang up.

I absolutely dread telling Ellen I have to leave early, especially when it's not an emergency for my own family, but how do I leave Cory sitting in the nurse's office? I pack up my things and stop in Ellen's office, feeling a little sense of relief to find she's on the phone. Quickly, I jot her a note, slipping it on her desk before I head out the door.

The nurse greets me as soon as I walk in her office, thanks me for coming and walks over to Cory who is lying on a makeshift bed with his eyes closed, looking flushed and pale.

"How high is his fever?"

"It was 100.1 last time I took it. I gave him Tylenol, which was an approved medicine on his paperwork. I'm sorry to disturb you, but I couldn't reach his parents or Sherry."

"It's no trouble at all." I look over at Cory who is starting to wake up. "Hey, Cory, let's get you home. Where is your backpack?"

He points to the chair behind the door. I pick it up and hook one of the straps over my shoulder. Cory gets up and follows me toward the door, telling me he feels nauseous. When we get to the car, I have him sit in the back and give him a plastic bag in case he throws up.

No one is home when we get to his house. I try calling Karen again, and again it goes directly to voicemail, and since I have already left three messages, I hang up, then try calling her husband's office. His secretary answers and in a very crisp, practiced tone she informs me he is in a meeting. I ask her to interrupt him, explaining that his son is sick and running a fever in the backseat of my car while his wife is MIA. She puts me on hold and a few minutes later, Jerry is on the line. He tells me he isn't sure where Karen is, but he will come home. It should take him about twenty minutes, but there is a spare key in the flowerpot by the front door.

I find the key and once Cory is comfortable on the couch, I go into the kitchen to get him some ginger ale and crackers to try to settle his stomach. I am so familiar with this house and yet I feel extremely uncomfortable being here. Cory drinks the ginger ale and says he feels a little better. I turn on the TV for him and hand him the remote, then realize I am going to be late picking up Sean, so I call Abby and she says she will get him and drop him off at my house. He has a key so he can let himself in and wait for me.

I'm getting impatient and more than a little irritated while I wait for Jerry. Finally, he walks in the door, thanking me profusely. When I ask where Karen is, he looks embarrassed. She and Sherry had a spa day and probably turned off their phones. I nod, tell Cory I hope he feels better, collect my things, and start toward the door.

I have my hand on the handle, about to leave, when Jerry says, "I really can't thank you enough. Given everything that's happened over the last few years, I wouldn't have blamed you if you said no."

I turn to face him, and he looks apprehensive. "You know me, Jerry. That's not how I roll, and I certainly wouldn't do that to Cory. I wish I could say Karen would do the same, but we both know the truth." Then I turn around and leave with my head held high.

That night after Sean goes to bed, I tell David what Jerry said. He shakes his head and says, "I know you and I know you have this incredible sense of loyalty, but you really do have to learn to say no. It hurts me when I see people take advantage of you."

Just as he says that a message comes through on my phone. I see Karen's name pop up. The message I open floors me. "Thank you for helping Cory today. It was an error on the part of the school. They had the wrong form. I made the correction and removed you as emergency contact."

Really? That's the thanks I get? I look up at David with tears in my eyes and say, "Lesson learned. From now on I will be more selective about who I say yes to."

He takes my phone and reads the message.

"You do know the problem is with her, right? She obviously has issues, and they have nothing to do with you. Do you still want to go to the bar mitzvah? We can cancel and do something fun with Sean."

"I don't want to go, but I don't want to disappoint Sean. I wish we could drop him off, but I don't think he'd be welcomed by himself."

"Let's talk to him tomorrow. Maybe he will surprise us."

In the morning Sean says exactly what I anticipated he would say. "Of course I want to go. Our whole bar mitzvah class will be there."

I feel gloomy the rest of the morning. I work out and barely make it through my yoga class. On my way home the rep calls and sets a date for our CGM training which perks me up a little. Maybe my reward for my good deed will be a few nights of sleep. One can hope.

Thirty-six

I'm putting away groceries when David calls from work to tell me he has big clients coming to town and would like us to take them out to dinner. I mark down the date and as soon as we hang up, my phone rings so quickly that I answer without looking at Caller ID, assuming it's David calling back. Naturally, I'm quite startled when I hear Sherry's voice, and she wastes no time getting right to the point of her call. To my surprise, she asks if I can meet her the next day for coffee. When I remind her that I work on Wednesdays, she is persistent and asks about Thursday, emphasizing that she has something important to discuss and would rather not do it over the phone. My curiosity gets the better of me, so I agree to meet her on Thursday after drop-off.

Thursday morning, I drop Sean off and drive to Java Hut, feeling apprehensive as I approach the door. I spot Sherry sitting at a corner table, so I get in line to order my latte and sit down in the chair opposite her. She smiles at me, and I return the smile, but I feel my guard going up.

"What's up?" I ask. Might as well pull the Band-aid off.

"How have you been?" Sherry asks.

"Sherry, after all this time, I don't think you asked me here to make small talk. What's going on?"

"I'm a little surprised you came. I don't know where to start."

I sit back and patiently wait, knowing I'm not making this easy. I'm so hurt over what's happened the last few years and David's warning, "Proceed with caution," is playing like a broken record in my head.

Sherry's eyes fill with tears. "I owe you a tremendous apology. I am just so sorry for the way I've acted since Sean was diagnosed and I want to fix it, but I don't know how. I miss you, I miss our friendship, and I have so much regret for the way I've behaved."

"Why don't you start by telling me what happened to us. Because I haven't got a clue why you both pulled away from me."

"It really was a snowball effect. When Sean was diagnosed, Karen and I were shocked. I wanted to help but didn't know how. I was also scared. Then Karen started filling my head with all these scenarios of things that could go wrong for Sean, and I let her convince me that we shouldn't be alone with him because it was too much responsibility. When we planned those trips, she said he would hold our boys back and it was better for them if we went on our own. It was easier to go along with her at the time, but I realize now what a huge mistake that was."

I'm trying to digest what she is saying.

"What made you decide to tell me all this?" I ask cautiously.

"Two things. First, when you picked up Cory from school when he was sick, I was reminded of how unselfish you are. Even with the way we treated you, when Cory needed you, you were there. I'm embarrassed that I wasn't there for you." She pauses, trying unsuccessfully to blink away the tears in her eyes.

"And the second thing?"

"Do you remember my sister Evelyn?"

"Of course. Is she ok?"

"Her daughter was diagnosed with type 1 diabetes two weeks ago."

My mouth drops open, and I move my hand to cover it as I wince. "I'm so sorry, Sherry. Is her daughter ok?"

"Yes, she is now. I flew out there to help with her other kids so she could focus on Rachel. Staying with her for that first week was eye-opening. I had no idea what you went through, how difficult it was to manage everything. She is shattered and exhausted. I thought back to the weekend we went to Nashville. When we got delayed going home, I thought you would laugh along with us, but you were so uptight and annoyed. It wasn't until I saw what my sister was dealing with that I understood the courage it took for you to keep our plans and the panic you must have felt being away from Sean. I was so insensitive. I'm just so ashamed of myself for turning my back on you."

"Sherry, I don't know what to say. I think I need to process everything. There's still a lot of hurt there for me."

"I understand. Take as much time as you need. I just hope you know I'm sincerely sorry and I want to try to mend our friendship. I miss you very much. Also, just so there are no surprises, I asked Karen to seat us together at the bar mitzvah. Are you still going?"

"Yes. It's important to Sean and I never wanted our issues to affect how he felt about his friends." I glance at the clock and realize that if I don't leave now, I'll be late for another appointment.

I pick up my purse and coffee cup and stand to leave. "I'm truly sorry about your niece. If Evelyn wants someone to talk to, feel free to give her my phone number. For the last few years, I've been mentoring newly diagnosed families through that initial adjustment period. I'm happy to be there for her if she wants to call. I would highly suggest she reach out to her local Breakthrough T1D office. She will need a lot of support."

Thirty-seven

It's Cory's bar mitzvah day, and the moment we enter the synagogue, Sean leaves us to sit with Billy and their other classmates. As we take our seats toward the back, Karen turns and nods at me, so I acknowledge the gesture with a slight wave of my hand. Our days of smiles and hugs are long gone. I see Sherry and Richard across the aisle, and we wave as David and I open our prayer books. After services Sean runs into the social hall with his friends to eat. When David and I find an empty table and sit down, Sherry and Richard immediately walk over and ask if it's ok if they join us. Having offered to watch their things while they get their food, I look around the room, searching for that old, familiar feeling of belonging, but it's nowhere to be found in this space.

That evening, the DJ has the crowd on the dance floor from the moment we enter the ballroom, which is decorated to the nines. Keeping with the theme of outer space, they have recreated the solar system, which is hanging from the ceiling. The centerpieces are spaceships numbered Apollo One, Apollo Two, all the way up to number fourteen. Mini spaceships with Cory's name on them are scattered along a large, U-shaped table, where the kids have assigned seats. As David and I make our way to the table, admiring the creativity of the decor, Sherry and Richard arrive, and Sherry places her bag on the seat next to mine. We exchange smiles as I ask Sherry how her sister is coping, and she tells me they are adjusting, but it's a slow process. I nod my head in agreement, knowing all too well. David and Richard get along as though they'd just seen each other yesterday, but I'm still very guarded with Sherry, so we talk about mundane things like what we've watched on Netflix and her latest book club selection.

The kids are back on the dancefloor playing games with the DJ while the adults eat dinner. I spot Sean in the crowd — he looks so happy to be with his friends. Billy has his arm around Sean's shoulder and Cory is on the other side of him. The music picks up again and David and I join Sherry and Richard on the dance floor. An hour later, I'm tired, so I excuse myself and return to the table. I'm contemplating which dessert I want when one of the girls from Sean's bar-mitzvah class runs over to me. "Mrs. Greene, come quick. Sean doesn't feel well." I jump up, grab the supplies I stashed under my seat and follow her to the other side of the room. Sean and Billy are sitting on the floor leaning against the wall. When Sean tests his blood sugar, and it reads thirty-five, I hand him glucose tablets and ask one of the kids to grab me some cookies off the dessert table. Once they deliver the cookies, I encourage them to go have fun but Billy says he wants to stay with Sean, so the three of us lean against the wall with Sean in the middle. As Billy entertains Sean with stories about his school, my gaze wanders to the dance floor and I see Karen staring at us. As soon as we make eye contact, she looks away.

Then I turn to my right and see Sherry coming towards us. Without saying a word, she sits down on the floor beside me and rubs her shoulder up against mine. We don't talk, just sit silently. I'm trying to hold back the tears, but they slide down my cheeks. Sherry hands me a napkin without saying a word. Sean and Billy have finished all the cookies, and I know in an hour Sean's blood sugar will be very high, but right now he is enjoying the moment with his friend, so I let it be. Once he is feeling better, they take off for the dance floor to catch up with Cory. A few more minutes pass, and we slowly get up, brush off our dresses and Sherry leans in and hugs me. I hug her back, thanking her for sitting with me.

Crossing the room toward my table, I'm not sure if it's real or imaginary that I feel Karen's eyes on me, causing my fury at God to bubble to the surface, competing with my distain for diabetes. Couldn't Sean have one day of fun without this stupid disease rearing its ugly head? And of all places, did it have to be at Cory's bar mitzvah, where Karen can witness our diabetes-induced time-out?

The more I think about it, the angrier I am with myself. Why do I always feel like I have to diminish what I am dealing with to make other people comfortable?

Thirty-eight

The week leading up to Sean's bar mitzvah is insanely busy. He has a final rehearsal with the rabbi, we're meeting the photographer for family pictures, and I have to run the welcome bags to the hotel for our out-of-town guests. Friday morning, in preparation for evening services, I stop by the synagogue and stuff baggies of glucose tablets around the seats on the bimah where Sean will be sitting with the rabbi during the service. I place some on the podium, where he will be reading the Torah, and then stash some under the seats where David and I will be sitting. Then I sit down in the empty sanctuary and have a talk with whatever higher being there is, hoping that if there is a God, my pleas are heard.

Dear God, if you are there, please, please, let things go smoothly this weekend. Please don't let any alarms go off during services. Please let Sean get a good night's sleep tonight and for the next forty-eight hours please let diabetes behave itself. I'm begging you, please don't take this moment away from him.

Saturday morning during services, I hold onto the CGM receiver for Sean and am ecstatic when no alarms sound. The pride I feel watching Sean on the bimah reading from the Torah and leading the congregation in prayers I've repeated my entire life, is beyond anything I could have imagined, and while I still can't muster up a connection to the words, the passing on of a tradition is not lost on me. The celebration that evening surpasses all my expectations. At one point during the night, I find myself on the dance floor with Abby and Valerie bopping around like fools, and when the DJ plays "Don't Stop Believin'," I notice Sherry nearby and instinctively grab her hand and pull her into our group. It was a perfect night, and when I finally crawl into bed, I immerse myself in a deep state of gratitude.

With the bar mitzvah behind me, I'm overwhelmed, juggling work, volunteering at Sean's school and co-chairing the gala with Valerie, leaving me little time for anything else. Abby joined the committee as decorating chairperson, which gives us an excuse to meet-up for lunch or coffee after our meetings. Sherry and I have kept in touch through text messaging, and while I'm treading lightly, if I'm being honest, I'm happy to have her back in my life.

Gala planning is coming to a head, and I'll be happy to put this event past us and focus on other things. David takes a sponsorship every year through his business, which includes a table for ten guests, and Valerie and Mike purchase their own table. We all fight over Abby, but I win, so she sits with us, then Valerie and I arrange the seating chart so our tables are next to each other. We raise the most money in the history of our gala, and while this is our fifth year participating, I still get choked up when they announce the grand total.

A few weeks later, we attend Sean's eighth grade graduation. David and I arrive early and hold seats for Valerie and Mike and Abby and Frank. Instead of wearing a cap and gown, the boys wear a jacket and tie and the girls wear dresses, all looking so grown-up, as they file onto the stage and take their seats. The principal of the middle school congratulates all the students on their achievements this past year and gives a speech about what they can expect next year moving into high school and the opportunities they will be exposed to. He encourages them to broaden their horizons and form new relationships. He tells them that some of their current friendships may change and that is a normal part of growing up. Valerie, Abby, and I look at each other. I know we are all hoping our boys stay close.

After the ceremony, we take the boys for dinner and listen to them make plans with each other for the summer. They are well past the camp stage, so keeping them busy will be a chore for us moms. I excuse myself to go to the ladies' room and Valerie says she has to go too. On the way, she leans close to me and asks, "Do you notice anything unusual about Mike?"

When I shake my head and reply "not really," she tells me he is becoming increasingly distant, more so than usual, but when she asks him if anything is wrong, he accuses her of creating drama where there is none and that she should focus on herself. Wow. I'm stunned into silence and wait for her to continue.

She chokes up a little when she whispers, "I don't know what to do. I'm so lonely and I can't get him to open up." I give her a hug and reassure her I'm here for her, always.

The High
School Years

Thirty-nine

The week before Sean starts high school we have our endo appointment. After meeting with Dr. Aronson, Denise comes in to talk to us. She sits down on the little stool and hands Sean a packet of papers. The cover page reads, "How to Drink Responsibly with T1D."

"Sean," she begins, "high school is full of exciting adventures and new challenges, and one of those challenges will be navigating your social life. I know you don't drink alcohol, but it's my job to prepare you in case you do. Of course, I have to remind you that the legal drinking age is twenty-one, but we are realistic and want you to stay safe." She then spends ten minutes educating Sean on the effects of alcohol on his blood sugar and how to manage that if he does decide to drink. She emphasizes how important it is for him to tell the people he is hanging out with that he has T1D and to be sure that, if he is drinking with friends, they know that the symptoms of low blood sugar can mimic the behavior people display when drunk. Things like slurred speech, not walking straight, confusion or drowsiness can present as drunkenness but are also symptoms of low blood sugar.

"There's lots of good information in this packet, so look it over and keep it as a reference. If you have any questions after reading through it, we can discuss them at your next appointment, and you can always email me."

Sean nods and I thank Denise. I'm so grateful they talk with the kids about this, but Denise has unknowingly added one more thing to my "things to worry about" list. The fun never ends.

The following Monday, Sean attends freshman orientation at Pine Brook Academy. He meets his teachers, gets his locker, and then participates in a scavenger hunt to get familiar with the layout of the high school. Pine Brook is a smaller magnet school and has a tradition of taking the freshmen on an overnight field trip so they can all bond before classes start. This will be Sean's first field trip without David chaperoning, and it's also the first time he has spent the night away from us since his diagnosis. Up until now, I have still been filling his insulin reservoir for him on site change days. It's the one thing I can do to help him, and so I do it happily. But because he will be on his own overnight, I make him practice filling it by himself the day before he leaves. He resists at first, but I make it clear that if he doesn't show me he can handle it, he can't go on the trip. That does the trick, and he agrees to do it himself.

By now, his CGM is more advanced, and David and I have an app on our phones that allows us to see Sean's blood sugar numbers. I breathe a little easier knowing I have access to that technology and when Sean's homeroom teacher gives me her phone number while confirming she has mine, it gives me a greater sense of relief. At drop-off, I am standing next to Valerie as we say good-bye to our boys. Abby is on the other side of the parking lot with Noah and I catch the smile on Abby's face as she hugs him. For a split second, I envy my friend and the ease at which she can let go. I hug Sean, trying to emulate the smile I witnessed on Abby's face as Valerie hugs John. The boys fist-bump their dads and step up onto the bus. As soon as the bus pulls away, Valerie takes my hand and she's shaking. I feel a little tremor myself.

"This is hard."

I nod and squeeze her hand because I don't trust myself to speak.

That night I wake up every few hours and check my app to make sure his numbers are good. By the morning I'm feeling confident he is doing well, so I pack my things and leave for work. But, when I'm stopped at a red light, my phone starts alarming. I pull over into a nearby parking lot, open the app and see Sean is at sixty with an arrow straight down. I try calling his teacher, but she doesn't answer. I wait a few minutes, thinking she will see a missed call, but I don't hear from her. Deciding I can't wait anymore, I dial Mr. Watson's cell phone number, knowing he is on the trip with them. He answers on the third ring, and I apologize for bothering him, then tell him why I am calling. As

I'm talking to him the app updates and is now displaying the number fifty-four with the arrow still straight down. He tells me Sean is eating and looks ok to him. He asks if I want to talk to him, but I decline. I prefer he doesn't know I called, especially because I don't want to embarrass him, I just need to know he is ok. Mr. Watson tells me not to worry, calmly assuring me he will go over to Sean and make sure he is ok without him knowing I called.

I hang up, annoyed that I am now late, and hurry to work. At my desk, I monitor the app until I see the arrow turn around and his number rising to a healthy range. But as I look up, I notice Ellen standing in the doorway with her arms crossed across her chest, watching me with a look I would almost classify as annoyance meets pity. I quickly put my phone down and start to stand when she holds up her hand, signaling for me to sit as she approaches the chair across from my desk. She lowers herself into the chair as she gently asks if everything is alright. I nod, starting to explain, realizing as I try to describe this morning's scenario that I probably sound like a broken record at this point, always talking about Sean's blood sugar. Fearing I may be in danger of losing my job, I resign myself to whatever is about to happen. I stop talking and sit quietly, waiting for her to speak.

Ellen hesitates, then leans forward. "Jessie, I appreciate you and know how hard you work but lately it seems as if you are constantly distracted, arriving late or requesting time off for one thing or another. Are you sure this is where you want to be right now? Working and managing Sean appears to be a challenge."

I feel my lip start to quiver but refuse to give in to it. I look Ellen in the eye and say, "Ellen, I realize there are times when I have had to leave or take time off to care for Sean, but I always get my work done and I've never let anything fall through the cracks. I'm sorry if it seems like I'm not as present as you feel I should be, but believe me when I say I take my responsibilities here seriously and I don't want to lose my job."

"Jessie, you are one of my best employees and I don't want to lose you, but I also don't want to feel like this job is contributing to any additional stress you may have. I trust you will tell me if it gets to the point where you can no longer manage both." She gives me a long, level look, gets up and leaves my office.

The first chance I get, I call Valerie and tell her what happened. Now it's my turn to fall apart, unloading all my stress in one large breath. "I feel like such a failure at work, like I've become the person who is no longer reliable because I never know from one minute to the next what this ridiculous disease is going to require. Ellen's right, I am often distracted, like this morning, the minute that CGM alarm went off and I couldn't reach his teacher, I started to panic, envisioning all kinds of crazy scenarios. It was all I could think about"

I take a gulp of air and continue my rant. "Valerie, how are we going to send them to college in four years? Who is going to look out for them?"

Valerie's calm voice soothes me as she talks me off the ledge, because that is what we do for each other. If we ever fall apart at the same time, I'm not sure who will put us back together. Once I've calmed down, we confirm our plans to meet Abby for dinner before heading over to the school to wait for the buses to arrive that evening. Hanging up, I try to focus on my work, but the day is basically shot for me, so I organize my files and watch the clock until I can leave the office.

Later that evening, Valerie, Abby and I are leaning against my car in the school parking lot and I am flooded with relief when Sean steps off the bus with a smile on his face, followed by John and Noah. The boys rush to us and are talking over each other, gushing about what a great time they had. When we get home, David and I sit down with Sean, who is completely unaware of the stressful morning I had watching his low blood sugar from afar. We take a moment to enjoy his stories and then talk about putting a plan in place so we don't worry and panic, explaining how important it is that when he is away from us and experiencing a low, he must text a thumbs-up so that we know he is aware and taking care of it. It's our next step in him taking full responsibility for his diabetes and earning our trust, which I am just realizing is going to be a long, winding road.

Forty

On my day off, I'm trying to get chores done when I get a call from the nurse telling me Sean is running a fever, so I drop what I'm doing and head over to the school. When I get there, he is pale and can barely keep his eyes open, so I run him over to the doctor's office, where he tests positive for the flu. After I bring him home, I call David and give him a list of things we need from the pharmacy, including sugar-free Gatorade to keep him hydrated. Diabetes is relentless, causing me to dread the next few days, as it is so hard to manage T1D when Sean is sick. Already, his blood sugar is running high and, while Sean keeps administering insulin through his pod, we can't get his numbers down. We continue increasing the insulin and I am constantly on the phone with Denise, confirming we are following proper protocol, leaving me on edge the entire time he runs a fever. Thanks to the pump, I can manage his diabetes while he sleeps, which I do, allowing him to rest and get better. On the fourth day, his fever breaks and his numbers start coming down. On the fifth day, I finally sleep.

In the fall, since Sean and Noah both make the JV basketball team and John makes the lacrosse team,

Valerie and I start meeting in the parking lot midway through practice to visit and wait for the boys. And to be honest, I'm still anxious about the lows Sean deals with during practice, so I find comfort being close by. One afternoon, as we are sitting outside on the benches near the gym, Valerie tells me about a conversation she had with her sister-in-law. She, Mike, and John had gone to Atlanta to attend a party for her uncle's birthday at her brother Andy's house.

She starts setting the scene for me. "We were in the kitchen and I was helping Andy's wife Nicole decorate trays of food. We were having a nice conversation about her kids and then she asked me how John was doing. My usual answer is 'everything is good,' because they just don't get what we go through. But my guard was down, and I was exhausted because we had one of those nights when we were up several times treating a stubborn low. So, I said 'overall, he's good, but nights like last night wipe me out.' And then I told her what we went through."

I'm nodding along because I know just where this is going and my heart hurts for my friend.

"Andy was walking into the kitchen just as Nicole, in a condescending tone, said 'Really, Valerie, John is in high school. Why are you still getting up with him at night?' I glanced over at Andy to see if he would jump in and defend me, but he grabbed a carrot, started chomping on it and nodded along with her."

"So how did you respond to her?"

"I said, 'Nicole, John deals with this all day, every day and will for the rest of his life. If one of your children was sick in the middle of the night, would you leave them to fend for themselves because they are old enough? I get up with him because this disease is exhausting and he shouldn't have to deal with it all by himself, no matter how old he is. Until you walk in my shoes, don't you dare judge me for how I care for my child."

"Good for you, Valerie. What did Andy say, and where was Mike?"

"Andy just kept chomping on his carrot, staring at me like I'd lost my mind. I'm sure they think I'm an overprotective, helicopter parent. If they only knew the restraint we show every day, giving our boys their independence and at the same time making sure they're healthy and safe. It's exhausting. As for my wonderful husband, Mike stood there, watched the exchange like it was a tennis match and then sighed and left the room."

I put my arm around her, and we sit quietly for a few minutes. I'm thinking about all the times I attempt to step back and allow Sean his independence, realizing that as hard as I try, I'm not always successful at letting go. He has no idea that I sit outside his basketball practice *just in case*, or that I still wake up in the middle of the night to check my app, not to mention the times I administer his insulin during the night when his number is too high. I just can't put that burden on him yet. Afterall, I'm a grown adult with the ability to rest during the day if I need to. He is a growing boy who needs to be alert and rested to go to school.

"People have no idea the effort it takes for our boys to function throughout the day while managing the highs and lows of T1D. You really have to live it to understand it. But we know what they accomplish and how hard they work to manage it. If we can relieve some of their burden for them, we will do it over and over again."

Valerie nods her head in agreement and wipes away a few tears. "It's just disappointing. You would think family is a safe place, but I felt so judged."

"I understand exactly how you felt, my friend. You're a great mom raising an amazing son. Don't let anyone make you feel less than."

The next day, when I'm at the gym finishing my workout, my phone rings. Caller ID identifies Hope. On my ride home I return the call and she asks if I can meet with her that afternoon. Later, when I walk into her office, I'm pleasantly surprised to see Valerie sitting in front of her desk, which piqued my curiousity.

"Hi, ladies," I say as I put my purse down and take the chair next to Valerie.

Hope is never one to waste time, so she immediately gets to the point. "I asked you both here because I have an exciting opportunity that I wanted to run by you.

Breakthrough T1D has been invited to testify in front of the Congressional Diabetes Caucus on Capitol Hill to encourage the government to allocate more money for type 1 diabetes research. The caucus' main responsibility is to gather and share knowledge about diabetes with members of Congress and their staff while providing support of legislative activities that improve diabetes research, education and treatment. My ask is simple. Would you both be willing to go to Washington and meet with the committee to share your stories? Advocacy work is so important, and this could really impact their decision to continue their support."

I'm flabbergasted. "Why us?" I ask.

"Because you both have compelling stories to tell about your journey parenting boys with T1D, not to mention the effort you put into raising awareness in the community. You fully understand the importance of funding research to advance treatments and cure this disease. I can't think of better representation."

Valerie and I look at each other and grin. We tell Hope we will check the dates she gave us with Mike and David and get back to her tomorrow.

That night at dinner, after Sean shares stories from his day and David fills us in on some office gossip and a marketing idea he has for a new client, I announce, "I have news. I've been invited to represent Breakthrough T1D in Washington and testify in front of the Diabetes

Caucus." I give them all the details about why we are testifying and my schedule. We leave on a Tuesday, testify on Wednesday and will be back home by dinner on Thursday night. They both are so excited for me, and David immediately marks his calendar to block the dates so he can get Sean to and from school.

I call Hope the next day to say I'm in. I know Valerie called her first thing this morning to say she is a yes too. I'm so motivated and wish it weren't a month away.

The following week we have our gala meeting. It's coming along great, and I believe this may be our biggest year yet. Sponsorships are up from last year and we have already exceeded our attendance goal with tickets purchased. The volunteers in charge of decor share their vision with the committee, and everyone agrees it's going to look amazing in the ballroom. When we are discussing our speaker lineup, I suggest that Valerie give the keynote speech this year, and Hope thinks it's a great idea. I'm delighted when Valerie agrees.

Later that day I meet Sherry for lunch. We catch up on the boys and she fills me in on synagogue gossip. Since resigning my position as sisterhood president, I am not as "in the know" as I used to be, and I must confess, while I don't miss it, I do like hearing the gossip. I don't ask about Karen, and Sherry never mentions her. I assume they are still friends, but we just don't go there. As we leave, she asks if David and I would like to have dinner with her and Richard Saturday night, so we pick a restaurant and hug goodbye.

Saturday night we meet Sherry and Richard at Calista's Italian Bistro. The conversation flows just like old times, and over dessert, Sherry asks a lot of questions about Breakthrough T1D because she is very interested in volunteer opportunities. David invites them to join us as guests at our table this year so they can experience the gala, which they enthusiastically accept before he can even finish telling them the details. Sherry is so excited that Monday morning she texts me pictures of several dresses and wants my opinion on which one to wear. I send her a picture of my dress and ask her if she wants to go get her hair and makeup done with me the day of gala and she immediately texts back YES. I've finally let my guard down with her, although I don't confide in her like I used to.

Forty-one

As chairperson, I'm expected to welcome everyone to the ballroom, so once the emcee introduces me, I walk onto the stage, thank the gala committee, reading off all their names, and then remind everyone why they are there and implore them to please give generously.

After dinner and the live auction, Valerie takes the stage, and the room is so quiet you could hear a pin drop on the carpet.

"Good evening," she begins. "My name is Valerie Walker. My son John was diagnosed with type 1 diabetes at the age of seven." She goes on to share her story and by the time she finishes, tears are flowing throughout the ballroom. The crowd is on their feet cheering as Valerie wipes away her own tears and makes her way to her table. I run over and hug her. "You were amazing tonight. I'm so proud of you, my friend." I rush back to my table as the auctioneer begins asking for donations. He opens the floor at $75,000 and immediately two donor cards are in the air. Bid cards are flying left and right as the auctioneer announces each level. By the time they tally the donations and Hope takes the stage to announce how much we've raised, I'm on pins and needles. The total leaves me breathless. We have exceeded our goal by $200,000. The audience erupts with applause and David wraps his arms around me cheering so loudly I think I may lose my hearing. I'm grinning from ear to ear and tears are streaming down my face. *Please, please let this make a difference.*

I'm still on a high from the gala the following week when Valerie and I leave for Washington. We attend a dinner and research update the night we arrive that includes volunteers from across the country who have scheduled meetings with their local representatives. When we walk into the ballroom, I'm astounded by the amount of people present and spend time meeting other volunteers who either have T1D or are parents of a T1D child. During the research update, we learn about a new product that should be hitting the market in the next few years. It's called an artificial pancreas. The premise is that the CGM communicates with the pump, and based on the blood sugar readings, the pump regulates the amount of insulin that is dispensed. It sounds very sci-fi to me and as much as I try to visualize how this will work, I can't. But when I talk to David after the presentation, he tells me he's been reading about the clinical trials and is very optimistic it will make life so much easier for Sean. He reminds me that these trials take a long time, and it will be a few years before these devices are approved for use.

In the morning, we board buses that take us to Capitol Hill. As I step off the bus, my eyes travel up the stairs toward the entrance of that sacred building and I am overcome with emotion. Today I will use whatever power I have to convince our lawmakers to continue funding research for type 1 diabetes. Walking through the hall on our way to the meeting room, I remind myself of all the important decisions that are made at the Capitol every day and the impact they have on all of us. Then we are led through double doors into the chambers where Valerie and I will tell our stories.

Valerie is first and, after sharing the story of John's diagnosis, she talks about her frustrations and the difficulties of managing T1D, wrapping up her testimony by addressing her concerns for John's future. When it's my turn, I tell them about the first time I had to give Sean a shot and how frightening it was. I share with them how the pump improved Sean's quality of life and give them a few examples of the positive impact it has on his life. Then I tell them about the CGM and what a game-changer it has been because finally we could fall asleep knowing that if Sean's blood sugar was in danger of going low or running too high, an alarm would alert us before it reached a danger zone. I share with them my belief that some of the worst situations tend to bring about the greatest blessings, whether it's the people they bring into your life or the chance to make a difference in somebody else's life. Then I implore them to make that difference by funding research so that we could improve on the technology and treatments available and maybe, just maybe, their support will lead to a cure.

On the plane ride home, Valerie and I relive the highlights of our trip. It's been a whirlwind month between the gala and our trip to Washington. I'm ready to get home and let things settle down. School lets out in a few weeks and all I want is a cool beverage, a good book and a sunny day by the pool.

Forty-two

Melanie has hired Sean, Noah, and John as camp counselors so they will be busy weekdays, leaving me to focus
all my attention on work and my family. The night before
camp starts, I watch Sean organize his backpack and am
relieved when he includes his back-up test meter and
glucose tablets without a reminder. Now that he has his
own phone and we have the CGM app, I feel a little more
relaxed, although I'm always half-listening for the alarm.

Abby offers to drop the boys off Monday morning
and, since Ellen closed our office for the week, we are
spending the day at my neighborhood pool. I'm packing
up a cooler of snacks and drinks for us when I look down
and see a puddle of water coming from under the refrigerator. When I open the door, it feels unusually warm
inside. I glance up at the top shelf where I keep Sean's insulin and start to panic when I remember I had just refilled
his prescription so there are ten new vials that must stay
refrigerated. I don't give a thought to the fact that I also
just stocked the refrigerator with food for the week. All I
can think about is saving the insulin. I call my neighbor
to the right, and they aren't home. I call my neighbor to

the left and the husband answers. I don't know them well. Ours is a cordial wave-when-we-see-each-other relationship but I'm desperate. I ask him if I can store the insulin in his refrigerator and he apologizes and says he would love to help but they are packing to leave town for a two-week vacation. I thank him anyway and hang up. I would call Valerie, but I know she is having coffee with a newly diagnosed mom. I dial the only other person I can think of who lives close by, and thankfully, Sherry answers on the second ring.

Before she even has a chance to say hello I launch right in. "Sherry, I need a big favor. My refrigerator broke. Can I store Sean's insulin in yours until we get ours fixed?"

"Of course. Come right over. I'll clear some space."

I hang up, quickly place the vials in a cooler with ice, text Abby to let her know what's happening and ten minutes later I'm at Sherry's house. She is waiting at the door, and I follow her into the kitchen. We place the vials of insulin on the top shelf of her refrigerator, Sherry reassuring me they will be safe there until I'm ready to pick them up. It's scary leaving the one thing that literally keeps my son alive out of my sight.

"Day or night if you need a vial, come right over. I don't care what time it is." Then she hands me a key and says, "Just in case I'm not home."

I hug her, thanking her profusely as I leave. When I get back home, Abby is waiting for me in the kitchen.

"I sure hope this isn't an omen for what our summer will be like." I laugh as Abby holds open the garbage bag while I throw out the items I know won't fit in the cooler.

I had planned on picking the boys up from camp but I'm now on stand-by, waiting for the repairman, so Abby says not to worry, she will pick them up. It really takes a village, and I am forever grateful for mine.

Later that day, the repair man confirms my suspicions. My refrigerator has died. First thing the next morning I drop the boys at camp and drive straight to the appliance store, where I pick out a new one. Most people purchase appliances based on the features they offer, but I buy based on stock availability in their warehouse. After I place the order, I turn on all my charm and beg the salesperson to expedite delivery, explaining how crucial it is. He plays around with the computer for what feels like an eternity, but in fact is only five minutes, then looks up and tells me it's my lucky day — he can deliver it late that afternoon. Feeling both fortunate and very relieved, I head to the gym to release my frustrations on that poor elliptical machine.

A few hours later they call to tell me delivery is scheduled between three and five p.m., so I call Valerie and ask her if she can pick up the boys, unhappy to be imposing on her again. But, I push that aside and thank her for being so flexible, then hang up and text Sherry with the delivery update and ask if I can come by in the morning to pick up the insulin. She responds immediately, "Of course. I'll be here."

My new refrigerator comes and once it's installed, I wipe it down and place a thermometer inside. I don't ever want to be caught off guard again. As it is, I'm worried about how the insulin I had stored held up. I don't know how long the temperature was off in the refrigerator before I noticed the leak. It finally reaches optimal temperature, so I load up whatever I rescued from my old fridge and then go to the grocery store.

When I get home, Sean is in the kitchen having a snack. While he helps me bring in the groceries, he tells me about his day and about the other counselors. One girl's name keeps popping up in his stories. He smiles when he mentions her, and I try to hide my pleasure because I think he has his first crush. He tells me some of the counselors are making plans for the weekend, getting together at someone named Nick's house to go swimming. Would it be ok if he went? He mentions that John and Noah are invited too. I say yes, realizing we are entering a phase where he will be hanging out with kids I don't know, whose parents I don't know.

That night I get a group text from Valerie to me and Abby. "Does anyone know who Nick is?" I respond "no" but Abby writes back, "Yes, he lives down the street from us. Nice kid, nice family. All good."

Sean is having the best summer with his friends. We

host them all at our pool for a pizza party and I notice that when Sean and John take their shirts off to go swimming, they are completely uninhibited and not one person comments on their insulin pods or the CGMs they wear on their stomachs. We raised Sean to be proud and not hide his diabetes, but it makes me feel good to see how his new friends accept him and John just as they are. Karen flashes through my mind, and instead of the anger I used to feel when I thought of her, I feel pity. Her actions cost Cory a really good friendship.

Forty-three

At the end of the summer Sean and I shop for school clothes, which is a big wakeup call that time is moving along, as he has gotten so tall that nothing in his closet fits him. I can't believe he is starting his sophomore year of high school. During the first week of school he brings home a packet from the guidance counselor, advising that they will begin college counseling mid-year, and he has some forms he needs to fill out so they can get to know him better. As a family we have been assigned an appointment in January to meet with his college counselor, Garrett. Also included in the packet is a permission slip for a field trip to visit a large state university and a small liberal arts campus so they can get a feel for the differences.

I'm meeting Valerie and Abby for lunch, and as soon as we are situated and the waitress takes our order, we start talking about the college packet the boys brought home. Abby is full of energy, talking about all the schools Noah wants to explore. Valerie looks like I feel, which is a little nauseous. While Abby goes on and on, I reach under the table and squeeze Valerie's hand. She nods at me with a little smile and we both turn our attention back to Abby. It's not that I'm not excited, because, truly, I am. It's that I still haven't come to terms with the reality that Sean will not be down the hall from us at night and that if something happens, I won't be right there to help him. I feel an overwhelming sense of urgency to make sure he is completely prepared to take care of himself and is confident in how to handle any situation that may arise.

But before I can even think about preparing him for college, I have to prepare myself for something even more daunting. In our state you can get your beginner's driving permit at the age of fifteen and your license at sixteen. Sean is turning fifteen in the fall. David and I discuss it and agree we won't bring it up. If Sean does, we will deal with it, but we think fifteen may be too young and we want to wait until he is ready to take on that responsibility.

We happen to have our quarterly visit with Dr. Aronson the week of Sean's birthday. David joins us for the appointment, which he rarely does anymore, but he has some questions about the artificial pancreas. We have heard they are in clinical trials and are eager to learn more, hoping that it will be available before Sean goes to college. Dr. Aronson is very knowledgeable about the latest clinical trials and while they are promising, it still looks like we are several years away from the artificial pancreas going to market. Which means it probably won't be available to Sean before he starts college. He does tell us that there is a more advanced version of the CGM Sean wears, including an easier application process than his current CGM. He updates all Sean's prescriptions and includes one for the newer version he mentioned. He makes a few changes to Sean's pump settings, and I think we are about to wrap up this visit when Denise walks in. Dr. Aronson shakes David's hand as he leaves while Denise turns to Sean. "Happy birthday, Sean." she says with a smile.

Sean returns the smiles and says, "Thanks."

"Sean, I'm sure you know that once you turn fifteen you can apply for your beginner's driving permit. Have you given it any thought?"

He shakes his head and says, "Not really. I guess I've been busy with school and getting ready for basketball try-outs. I hadn't thought about it."

David and I look at each other. I'm a little surprised. Most boys are counting down the days until they can drive.

"There's no rush, Sean. Whenever you're ready, let me know and we'll talk about how to manage diabetes and driving. There are some protocols you will need to follow, but we can go over all that when the time comes."

In the car ride home Sean is quiet and I'm a little relieved. I sense that he is hesitant to take on that responsibility right now, and I'm ok with that. I don't believe in rushing kids into doing things just because everyone else is. They have to be ready to take those steps and I just don't think he is there yet. When I share this with Valerie later, she tells me John is having the same reaction. He seems ambivalent about driving and she is not pushing it. Noah, on the other hand, is already pushing Abby to sign him up for driving lessons, even though his birthday is still three months away.

To celebrate his birthday, Sean has invited a group of his school friends over for pizza and a movie. Of course, he includes Noah and John. After the boys eat, they head to the family room to watch their movie. I bring up bowls of popcorn and set up snacks in the room for them, then join David on the back deck. We're chatting about nothing in particular, when David throws me a curveball by telling me how much he misses going to synagogue with me. We've attended services sporadically since Sean's bar mitzvah, but I'll admit I make a lot of plans on the weekends that don't include going to services. David makes it clear he misses that part of our life and says he wants to start going on a more regular basis. Once again, I try explaining how detached I feel from the prayers and the people when I am there and that sitting in services doesn't bring me any peace. Our conversation is getting very heated as we talk in circles, not really hearing each other, until I notice someone in the kitchen. Hitting pause on the conversation, I step inside.

"Noah, is everything ok?"

"Yes. I told Sean I would get his glucose tablets for

him. He's starting to go low." He reaches into the cabinet and grabs the bottle.

"Thank you, Noah. You're such a good friend to Sean," I tell him, as he turns to go back upstairs.

He shrugs and replies "Sean's a good friend to me." I watch him run up the stairs and once again I am filled with gratitude for the people in Sean's life.

When I turn around, David is standing behind me. He looks sad and now I feel guilty. "What do you want me to do?" I ask him.

"How about we start with attending services once a month, and if you still feel the same way, maybe you can speak to someone to help you work through whatever this is that's holding you back."

In an exasperated tone, I ask "Who would I even talk to about this?"

Tentatively, David asks, "The rabbi?" I don't answer him. I just shrug my shoulders and agree to go to synagogue with him, feeling conflicted between my inclination to ignore the issue and my desire to please my husband.

Friday rolls around and we attend services. David does so much for me, that I want to show up for him. While I don't feel as numb as I have felt in the past few years, I still don't find myself at peace, and struggle to come to terms with this shift in my connection to a space that was a second home to me for so long. Later that night, I tell David

I am calling the rabbi next week to schedule a meeting. I owe it to him and to myself to try to work this out.

True to my word, I make an appointment and Tuesday morning I find myself sitting in the rabbi's office with sweaty palms and mild skepticism. She listens intently as I describe my conflicted feelings about attending services, how empty I feel when I'm in the synagogue and how angry I am toward this higher being I have prayed to my entire life. I express how betrayed I felt after Sean was diagnosed and, while I've heard all the cliches about "bad things happen to good people," I don't understand a God that allows this to happen. Then I say the one thing out loud I haven't shared with anyone. "I don't know if I believe in God anymore."

She listens without interrupting and when I exhaust myself, she kindly asks about my relationship with David, wondering if I ever get mad at him. "Of course, I do. You can't stay with the same person for as many years as we've been together without arguing or getting mad at each other."

She nods and says, "Every relationship has peaks and valleys. Feeling anger at times, especially in situations that are out of our control, is a healthy part of any relationship. We feel helpless and look to the person we hold in high esteem to take control for us during difficult times."

While I expected her to admonish me and tell me that God is ever-faithful and that my anger is misplaced, she surprises me by saying she understands.

"You have a relationship with God, and you feel like God let you down. There's a part of you, though, that is struggling with letting go. You're not ready to leave that relationship, evident in the fact that you keep coming back, yet you hold onto your anger, like a teenager digging in her heels, and it's manifesting itself through your disconnection to the prayers."

We sit quietly for a few minutes, and I let her words sink in. I look up when she carefully places her hand on mine. "Jessie, can I play devil's advocate for a minute?" When I nod, she asks, "What if God is actually the one guiding you through this ordeal? Consider for a minute the possibility that it is God lifting you up, providing you with inner strength and the courage to face the challenges that come your way. We all have times in our lives where we struggle and everyone faces scary situations, some life-threatening. Is it possible that our ability to face those dark times comes from God?"

She pauses to give me a chance to digest her suggestion, and, noticing that I'm hanging on her every word, she continues. She notes that in any relationship when you feel let down by someone you trust and put faith in, it's normal to have feelings of abandonment. Then comes the big BUT.

"How you choose to work through those issues will determine if that relationship is worth saving or letting go. Ultimately, only you can make that decision."

Forty-four

Over the next few days, I continue to revisit my conversation with the rabbi and surprisingly, I feel my anger dissipating. I don't know if I'll ever feel fully connected again, but I decide to focus on gratitude for the positives in my life. Slowly, I feel my grip loosen on the anger that I have held onto for too long now.

Feeling a little lighter, I prepare myself for our meeting with Garrett, the college counselor who will guide Sean through the application process. He is warm, welcoming and very knowledgeable, and while I think sophomore year is a little early to start this process, he emphasizes that now is the time to focus on building that "resumé." Based on Sean's current grades and the questionnaire he filled out, Garrett has printed a list of colleges he thinks may be a good fit for Sean. They are broken down into two categories; reach schools and safe schools. Garrett encourages him to start researching them, familiarize himself with their admissions requirements and be prepared to narrow down the list for their next meeting. He goes over the details of the field trip to visit colleges the following week and reminds us Sean must be on the bus by six-thirty in the morning.

I'm still thinking about our conversation with Garrett and trying to process how quickly this is all moving when I pick Sean up from basketball practice. I hand him a sandwich as he sits down in the passenger seat next to me. He's always starving after practice and can never make it home without eating. After a few bites, he glances over at me and says, "Mom, I want to apply for my driver's permit. Noah's birthday is next week and he's going to the DMV after school. Can I go with him and take my test?"

"What about practice? Do you want to wait until the season is over and I can take you?"

"I haven't missed any practices and I'm sure coach won't mind. If you want to come, that would be great. We can go with Noah and Abby. I have the driving manual from DMV and will study it this weekend. Also, I asked around and found out the name of the driving school my friends are using. I thought I could log some of my driving hours with an instructor and then I'll practice with you or dad before I can get my license."

Sean is so excited. I swallow my apprehension and say, "Well, you certainly have done your homework. I absolutely want to come with you. Afternoon, after school, works out great, since I won't have to take time away from work. Talk to Noah and let me know what day next week. Remind him you both have the field trip on Tuesday so any other day that week works for me."

As I look out at the road ahead of me, I can't help but notice how white my knuckles are from the tight grip I have on the wheel. *Here we go*, I think to myself.

The morning of the field trip we arrive at the school a little early. Sean hugs me good-bye, and I watch as he climbs the stairs onto the bus, sitting down next to Noah, with John in the row right behind them. I'm lost in thought when I feel two arms wrap around me from behind. I turn to see Valerie smiling through the tears in her eyes.

"Let's go. I have a morning coffee with a mom who is struggling with her son's T1D diagnosis. I'll meet you at the Breakthrough office for the outreach meeting this afternoon." I loop my arm through hers, and we start walking toward our cars.

Following the outreach meeting, where we planned a fun meet-up for newly diagnosed families, Valerie comes over to visit. I've tracked Sean's numbers throughout the day, and he's been all over the place with highs but never went too low. I'm sure being out of his routine isn't helping and who knows what they've been eating. We chat about the outreach program and how relieved we are that a new volunteer has stepped up to lead the committee. She was diagnosed at the age of seventeen and is now in her late twenties, with a little girl whom she watches like a hawk because she is petrified of her developing T1D. Valerie expresses how much these outreach programs helped her when John was first diagnosed and through these gatherings she learned so much from other parents — practical ways to deal with the literal highs and lows.

At dinner that night Sean talks nonstop about the colleges he visited. David and I ask him questions, which he answers willingly, expressing his preference for a bigger university over a small college. He likes the idea of having a football team to root for, and since his high school is relatively small, he wants to spread his wings and meet lots of different people, which we encourage wholeheartedly. We are caught by surprise, though, and don't offer any opinion when he mentions an interest in some out-of-state schools. That's a curveball we did not see coming. After Sean goes to bed, David and I have a heart-to-heart, agreeing that whatever school he chooses, no matter where it is, we will support him.

My nerves are already on edge one morning when I get a call from the company that supplies Sean with his insulin pods. We are on automatic shipment, so I'm shocked when they tell me the insurance company denied the refill because they require prior authorization. I'm baffled and think for sure this must be a mistake. I hang up and immediately call my insurance company and after an interminable twenty-minute hold, a care representative informs me that they now require an annual letter from the endocrinologist establishing medical necessity to fill this prescription. She tells me that a notice was sent to Dr. Aronson's office, but they have not heard back yet.

When I argue that we've been filling this prescription for a few years now, she stuns me into silence with her reply. "Does he still have type 1 diabetes?"

This nearly pushes me over the edge, but I find my voice, which I realize is very snippy, and my volume begins to rise uncontrollably as I respond, "Have you heard of a cure for T1D? Because if so, please share it with me. Otherwise, YES, HE STILL HAS DIABETES!"

I hang up and leave a message for Denise. I'm still fuming two hours later when she calls me back and assures me she has faxed over the paperwork, which was expedited and approved, and Sean's supplies will ship out this week.

I'm still feeling a little stressed when I pick up Abby before getting Noah and Sean from school to take them to the DMV. After they both pass their written tests, they break into a celebratory dance in the parking lot, laughing and high-fiving each other on the way back to the car. Abby whispers to me, "I'm so excited for them."

"Me, too," I say, although my excitement is tempered by my overactive imagination leading me to visions of sudden lows while driving that compound the anxiety every parent feels when their child starts to drive, taking mine to a whole other level. I attempt to silence my fears by focusing on my to-do list, which now includes arranging driving lessons for my very eager new driver.

I'm at work the next day, thinking that surely today will be better than yesterday, when my phone starts buzzing.

Caller ID tells me it's Sean and when I answer he tells me his pod failed, and he doesn't have another one with him. When I remind him we leave a supply at the nurse's office, he says she's not in her office and the door is locked. Trying to keep the frustration out of my voice, I tell him I'm on my way. I walk into Ellen's office to tell her I'm leaving, and she looks at me with an expression that I'm becoming too familiar with. "Really, again?" she asks.

"I'm so sorry, but I have to go help him. I'll be back as soon as I can."

Rushing home, I grab a pod and an extra vial of insulin and meet Sean, who is sitting in the office staring into space. I hand him his supplies and the receptionist offers him the use of the faculty bathroom so he has privacy. When he returns, he looks upset.

"Are you ok?" I ask, as I take back the insulin.

"I'm just annoyed. I was about to eat lunch, and just started to enter my carbs when the stupid pod starts beeping. It's so obnoxious. Everyone was looking at me, so I packed up my lunch and that's when I called you."

"I'm sorry that happened, Sean. Would you like me to sit with you while you eat?"

"No, I was starving so I ate the lunch meat without the bread. I'll have a snack on my next break. I have to get back to class. Thanks for helping me, Mom."

The receptionist looks up as he walks out and says "He's a great kid. One of my favorites."

Mine too, I think, but out loud I say, "Thank you."

By the time I get back to the office it's almost the end of my shift. I check in with Ellen and, sensing she is still annoyed with me, I hunker down at my desk and don't leave until I finish everything on my list.

Forty-five

Monday afternoon, I am driving all three boys home from school, and I can't help but eavesdrop, as the guys are talking in the backseat. John is telling Noah and Sean about a party someone is planning this coming weekend, and asking them to go with him. Noah seems hesitant and Sean doesn't really answer him. Trying to entice them, John mentions that the party is at Morgan Hansen's house. The little I know about Morgan is that she is friends with the "popular" girls, is on the school volleyball team and has an older brother in his senior year. If the rumors are true, their house is "the party house," and I debate interjecting, but decide to wait for Sean to bring it up before I say anything.

A few days pass and he still hasn't mentioned the party. But on Thursday, Valerie calls to ask me if I'm allowing Sean to go to Morgan's house Saturday night. She says John told her a few kids are meeting there, and he wants to go. "Sean hasn't mentioned it to me, so I don't think he's planning on it. Are you going to let John go?"

"I guess so. Some of his lacrosse friends are going and he really wants to go with them. Any thoughts?"

I hesitate and then decide it's not my place, so I say "No thoughts at all. I don't really know Morgan. She comes into the bookstore during my shift occasionally and is always polite but that's really all I know about her."

Valerie sighs. "I've heard some rumors about wild parties at her house involving her older brother. John thinks the only kids invited this weekend are his friends from school and some others from their grade. He also said he doesn't think her older brother will be home."

I'm relieved Valerie has also heard the rumors, so I don't have to be the one to tell her. As close as we are, we don't interfere in how we choose to handle situations with our kids.

"I'm sure he'll be fine. John's a good kid and if there's a problem, I'm sure he'll call you," I say, trying to reassure her.

Friday afternoon, I ask Sean what his plans are for the weekend. He mentions that he and Noah talked about getting together and asks if it's ok if Noah comes to our house. He doesn't mention John, so I don't ask about the party.

I'm fast asleep Saturday night when my phone rings. David and I jump up and I grab my phone, noticing the time is twelve-thirty and Valerie's name is scrolling across the screen. I hold my breath as I answer.

"Hey, what's up?"

Valerie is crying hysterically. Through gasps of

breath she says, "I'm so sorry to call you so late but I can't calm down."

"Slow down, Valerie. You can call me anytime. What's wrong?"

"I just had a big fight with John, which led to a bigger fight with Mike. I'm shaking I'm so upset. John went to that party tonight. Before he left, I reminded him to watch his blood sugar and begged him not to drink. Two hours after he left, I started getting alerts from his CGM that he was running high. At first, it was 300, then the arrow was pointing up and every five minutes when it updated, he was going higher and higher. Initially, I thought, he must have eaten and it would surely turn around. An hour later it wasn't even giving me a number, just reading HIGH, and the arrow was still diagonal up. I tried texting him and he didn't answer. I waited a few minutes and texted again. Finally, I found Morgan's information in the school directory and tried calling her mom. No answer. I tried her house phone and cell phone, and no one answered. Meanwhile, Mike was calling John's phone, but it kept going directly to voicemail. So we got in the car and we drove to Morgan's house. There were cars parked up and down the street, kids were hanging out on the front porch and the front door was wide open, providing me a perfect view of wall-to-wall kids holding red Solo Cups, which is when I freaked out. We walked into the house and finally found John sitting in their media room, because of course they have a media room. The minute he saw us he asked, 'What are you doing here?' and that made me even madder. I laid into him right then and there. I just lost it."

I've never heard Valerie like this and I'm bursting with questions but don't want to interrupt, so I let her continue.

"In front of all his friends I grabbed his cup right out of his hand, and drank it, which by the way, turned out to be plain seltzer. When I asked him what he was doing about his blood sugar and why he didn't answer any of our texts, he just stared at us, so I told him it was time for him to go and Mike and I turned to leave. He followed us to the car and the minute we got in the car he had the nerve to yell at us for showing up at his friend's party. Can you believe that?"

She doesn't wait for me to answer before she ramps it up again.

"I nearly jumped out of my skin, screaming, 'How dare you? Have you looked at your CGM? Do you have any idea how high you are and have been for the last few hours? We sent you text messages that were ignored. We tried calling you and it kept going to voicemail. We tried calling the house and no one answered. What the hell were we supposed to do?'

"Surprisingly, Mike interrupted me, trying to be the calm voice of reason, and asked John what he was doing that caused his number to go so high. He asked him point blank if he drank and John swore on his life he did not drink. By now we were calming down and I looked at the app and he was still close to 400 with a steady arrow, so I asked him again, 'What did you do?' and he shrugged his shoulders and said, 'I didn't enter my carbs when I ate pizza and a piece of cake.' I was speechless. Something in the way he said it and the look in his eyes broke me. He took out his pump and entered his carbs and the second we got home he went straight to his room and slammed the door.

"The minute John was out of sight, Mike started yelling at me that this was my fault. That I got him all worked up and that I shouldn't have assumed or accused John of drinking until I knew the facts and that I embarrassed his son in front of his friends. And then he stormed off and I'm sitting here feeling like a failure. But Jessie, I was so scared that something terrible would happen to him if his number didn't come down."

"Oh Valerie, what a horrible night."

"Jessie, I feel awful. But what else could I have done? Wait until they called me that he was having a stroke because his blood sugar was too high? How do I make things right with John?"

I'm completely shocked at Mike for his reaction, but I focus on Valerie and John. "Val, I think in the morning you have to talk to John, calmly. Ask him why he avoided entering his carbs and how he thinks you could have handled the situation. Hear him out. But keep in mind, he's a teenager. He's going to make mistakes. They all are."

We hang up and when I get back in bed David rolls over to face me and asks, "What was that all about?" I tell him the abbreviated version and we talk about Sean and how we imagine we would have handled it. But the truth is, I have no idea what I would have done in the same situation.

Forty-six

I don't hear from Valerie Sunday, so Monday after work I swing by her house. When she answers the door, she looks exhausted and frazzled. Following her into the kitchen, I take a seat at the table, while she fills the kettle for tea, then moves slowly around the kitchen, reaching for the tea bags and some muffins. When she finally sits down, I notice her hands shake as she places the steaming mug in front of me and hands me a napkin. I'm contemplating what to say when she starts talking.

"I took your suggestion. I sat down with John yesterday and apologized for my reaction when we entered the house. I told him I wasn't proud of the way I handled myself and was sorry I embarrassed him in front of his friends — that it wasn't my intention. Then I asked him if he just forgot to enter his carbs, and he said no, he didn't forget. He was with his friends, and everyone was eating and drinking, and he didn't want to take his pump out and enter his carbs in front of everyone. He was embarrassed by his diabetes. He explained that he had lowered the volume on his phone so if his pump alarmed, his friends wouldn't hear it. And then he put his phone in his backpack with his supplies. With the noise in the house, he never would have heard the alarms or phone ringing."

"Oh, Valerie. What a horrible experience for both of you."

Valerie grabbed some tissues from the box on the table and wiped her eyes. "The worst part is, I think he's really been struggling, and I didn't see it. He tells me he's burnt out and tired of dealing with it. And this whole time, I thought he was handling it just fine. He always seems so happy and easygoing. He's never mentioned feeling embarrassed by his diabetes before."

"You wouldn't know unless he told you. Is this the first time something like this has happened?"

Valerie nods her head yes.

"All we can do is support them the best we can. He's a teenager learning to navigate new social situations, and he's dealing with T1D on top of all that. He's going to make mistakes. Isn't it better he makes those mistakes while he still has the safety net of living at home? I'd rather Sean gets it out of his system now while I'm here to pick up the pieces."

Valerie nods again and sighs as she wipes away a few tears.

"Do you think he would benefit from talking to a therapist? Someone removed from the situation who can help him work through some of his feelings?" I ask with a little hesitation.

"I already thought about that. John said he's willing to try, so I called Denise this morning and she gave me the name of a counselor who's familiar with T1D. I'm waiting for them to call me back to schedule an appointment."

I'm nervous to ask but I do anyway. "How are things with Mike?"

"He's not talking to me. He said I made a bad situation worse, and I never should have reacted the way I did in front of John's friends. I haven't even had a chance to tell him about my conversation with John because he left the house yesterday morning to play golf and when he came home, we ate dinner in complete silence. And as soon as he was finished eating, he retreated to his office until he went to bed."

We sit quietly for a few minutes before Valerie says something I'm not expecting. "We've been having problems for a while now. We don't agree on how to handle certain situations. Mike doesn't like confrontation and would rather brush things under the rug than talk about them, whereas I can't let things go and feel the need to express what I'm feeling. It's been building and I think this weekend was the straw that broke the camel's back."

"I'm so sorry. I had no idea."

"I know. I try not to think about it. This will blow over and I'm sure things will go back to normal. Anyway, please don't mention anything to Abby. I'd rather just move on."

"Of course. I would never betray your confidence. I'm here for you, whatever you need."

Valerie walks me to the door and gives me a hug before I leave.

"Thanks for being such a good friend, Jessie."

"Right back at you, my friend. Go take a nap." I give her another hug and walk to my car.

On my way home I call David. After I tell him how John is struggling, we agree we should talk to Sean to make sure he is handling things ok, especially with the pressures of high school and all the social issues teenagers deal with. That evening, after we catch up on everyone's day, David starts the conversation.

"Sean, Mom and I were wondering how things are going for you at school?"

"Great. Grades are good," he answers through a mouthful of rice.

"What about socially? How are things going with your friends?"

"All good. Dad, what's up? What do you really want to know?"

"It's really that we want you to know that if you have issues at school or are struggling with diabetes, we are here for you. No judgment, just support."

I'm pretty sure I catch an eye roll. "I know that, Dad. And really, I'm doing well. Sure, I get frustrated with diabetes and it's a real pain in the neck, but it is what it is.

Nothing I can do to change it, so I try not to think about it. And my friends are cool with it."

"Are you ever embarrassed by it?"

"Not embarrassed. More annoyed. It gets in the way and sometimes I don't want to have to think about it. But I know I have no choice, so I just do what I need to do."

"Well, just know that if you ever want to talk about it, we are here. Don't keep things bottled up inside."

"I won't. I promise. Now can we talk about something else? Like my driving lessons?" He looks over at me with a look of anticipation when he says that.

"First lesson is scheduled for next Saturday."

"WOOHOO!" he yells, pumping his fist in the air.

Forty-seven

After Sean completes two driving lessons, David starts taking him out every night after dinner. They drive around the neighborhood, and if David is feeling brave, they venture out into town. About a month after his lessons start, Sean asks me if he can drive us to school in the morning. I agree he can do that, but I make my expectations really clear, which include testing his blood sugar or checking his CGM before getting in the car, and pulling over right away to test his blood sugar if he doesn't feel well. I've already stashed glucose tablets in the glove compartment and the center console between the driver's seat and the passenger seat. He agrees to all my stipulations and so, the following morning I'm sitting in the passenger seat as my son starts our car and begins to back down the driveway. *And we're off!* I think to myself, proudly watching him while he watches the road. My taxi driving days are nearing the end. It's a very bittersweet feeling.

Leaving him at school, I drive over to Java Hut to meet Abby for coffee. The conversation turns to our boys and Abby shares that Noah is talking more and more about college. He started making a list of some of his target schools and they are planning a trip this summer to take some tours. "Would you like to join us? We could ask Valerie and Mike too."

I've spoken with Valerie a few times. John started therapy and is doing much better. She and Mike are talking again, and things seemed to have calmed down for now, so I hope she agrees to go with us.

"That sounds like fun, and I'm sure the boys will love it. I'll talk to David tonight. Have you thought about the schools you want to visit first?"

She rattles off a few names and some of them are on Sean's list too, so I'm confident he will be excited to see them. That night at dinner I mention it to David and Sean and they both think it's a great idea, so I text Abby that "we're in."

Immediately, I get a message back. "Perfect. So is Valerie's family. Can you all come over Saturday and we can work out our itinerary? Dinner at my house, Saturday at six." It's followed by smiley faces and hearts.

The next morning, I call Valerie and she sounds out of breath when she answers the phone.

"Hey, what are you doing?"

"I decided to start running again. I'm tired of being in the gym."

"How's that working so far?" I ask, laughing.

"Well, I've made it a mile and I can't breathe, but other than that I'd say it's going great."

We both laugh and then I get serious.

"I wanted to check on you. How are you feeling?"

"I'm better. John has another session with the therapist next week and he's slowly opening up to me a little bit about his frustrations. Do you think he talks to Sean at all?"

"I'm not sure and I didn't want to ask. I don't know if Sean is aware of what happened, so I avoid bringing anything up. How are things with Mike?"

"Fine, I guess. I'm just so tired, Jessie."

"I get it. Hang in there, Valerie. Things will get better. John's a great kid, he just hit a slump. He'll come through this."

"Thanks. I'm going to hang up and try to run home now! I'll see you Saturday at Abby's house."

Forty-eight

The summer after sophomore year is all about hanging out with friends and once again the boys are working as camp counselors. Two weeks into camp, the boys are hanging out in my backyard when I overhear John mention a pool party one of the lacrosse players is hosting the following weekend and, since he can bring friends, he wants Sean and Noah to come with him. I get a little knot in my stomach. A while later, Sean comes inside and tells me about the party and asks if he can go with John. I ask him whose house it's at, and when he mentions the boy's name, I recognize it from volunteering in the school bookstore, so I tell him he can go.

But the night before the party, I sit down with Sean.

"There are a few things we need to talk about before this party tomorrow."

"Sure, Mom. What do you want to talk about?" He tries to cover an exasperated sigh, which I choose to ignore.

"First, I'm not sure if your friends are drinking yet, but if they are, I'm asking you to please not drink."

"Really, Mom? I don't drink. I don't want to drink. I swear, it won't be an issue."

"Good, I'm glad to hear that. Second, I want you to have a good time, but I also want you to be aware of your blood sugar. If you start getting alerts that you are running too high or especially if you are running low, I want you to text me a thumbs-up so I know you're aware. As long as I see that thumbs-up I won't bother you and I'll know you're taking care of things. But, just so we're clear, if I don't get the thumbs-up, I'm going to start calling you. And if I can't reach you, I'm going to come check on you. Neither one of us wants it to get that far. Agree?"

"Totally agree. That would not be cool. I'll text you if I'm going low. Are we done?"

"Done."

I go to my room and call Valerie to tell her about my conversation with Sean. She loves the thumbs-up idea and says she's going to use it as well. Once again, for a brief minute I envy Abby. I know she worries about Noah's safety, and underage drinking is a real issue of concern for her, but she is so much better at letting go, something I struggle with.

When I drop the boys off at the party on Saturday, I remind them Abby will be picking them up and call out, "Have a great time" as they run toward the house. Later that night, when Abby drops Sean off, he is tired but very talkative. He tells us who was there from school and then spills the beans that Noah likes one of the girls in their class. He begs me not to say anything to Abby or

Valerie so, after I cross my heart, he tells me more about her and how Noah keeps talking about asking her out, but the minute she talks to him, he chickens out. I take the opportunity to ask if he likes anyone special, but he just grins and shrugs his shoulders.

The week before our college tour trip, Abby, Valerie, and I get together for lunch. As we're talking through the details of our trip, I notice Sherry and Karen entering the restaurant. Sherry sees me and immediately waves, while Karen nods her head, and quickly turns to the hostess, who leads them to a table at the far end of the restaurant.

"Really," I say to my friends with a sigh. "After all this time, she can't just say hello? What the hell is wrong with her?" I'm surprised by how much it still upsets me. I know I need to just let it go because Karen will never change.

"I hear you," Abby comments, "but she's not worth the energy you put into thinking about her. In more interesting news, we are registered at University of Georgia, Clemson, Wofford and the University of South Carolina for official tours, which should lead to a fun-but-exhausting week." Our discussion revolves around SAT tutoring, on-line study guides and practice tests through a program the school is offering.

As we get up to leave, Sherry walks over. After saying hello to Abby and Valerie, she hugs me and says, "I've been wanting to call, but the end of the school year was so busy and time got away from me. Can we get together soon?"

"I'd love that. We'll be out of town all next week, so I'll call you when we get home, and we can make a plan." We hug again and as I turn to grab my purse, I see Karen watching me, so I smile and wave at her and walk out of the restaurant without looking back.

Forty-nine

Our college tours turn out to be so much fun and very enlightening. We start in Georgia, make our way to Clemson and then Wofford, ending our week in Columbia at USC. Each tour is unique and leaves us all with plenty to talk about, which we do every night at dinner. On the final day of the tour, we want to make the most of our last night together, so after touring the University of South Carolina, we walk around the city, exploring the Vista, and then make our way to Five Points for our last group dinner at Pawley's Front Porch, which came highly recommended and does not disappoint.

We're exhausted by the time we get back to the hotel, so we all go to bed early. But at two a.m. my phone rings. When I answer, Valerie says, "I'm so sorry to wake you. John's pump ran out of insulin and when he went to fill the new reservoir, he dropped the vial and it broke. Not only does our hotel room smell of insulin, but it was a brand-new vial, and we don't have a backup."

I am already out of bed and throwing on a pair of shorts. "I'm on my way," I say, as I grab our backup vial and my room key. When I meet her in the hallway, she looks completely drained and her eyes are brimming with tears. "Are you ok?" I ask, as I hand her the vial.

"I'm just exhausted. Every night it's something else. He's low, he's high, he's out of insulin. It just doesn't end. And to top it off, Mike conveniently reminded me that I packed John's supplies, so of course it's my fault we have no backup." Tears start to fall as I pull her in for a hug.

I find myself getting annoyed at Mike and it's getting harder for me to not express my true thoughts about him. "Valerie, I don't want to get between you and Mike, but it's no one's fault. We were only gone a few days, and you brought a full vial. It happens. I'm just glad we were with you, and I had a backup. Lesson learned for next time. You did nothing wrong."

"I appreciate that. I've got to get back to the room so John can change his site and go to bed. I'm really sorry I had to wake you." She gives me a hug and turns to leave.

"See you in the morning." I call out, as I push the elevator button.

As I'm crawling back into bed, David whispers, "Is John ok?"

I whisper back so I don't wake Sean. "Yes, he dropped his vial of insulin, and it broke. I gave them our backup vial, but that's not the real problem. I'm really worried about Valerie. Mike seems to blame her for everything."

David doesn't respond, he just pulls me closer to him, kisses my forehead, and immediately falls back to sleep. I can't stop thinking about Valerie, trying to imagine what I would do in her situation with Mike. Then my mind wanders to Sean and the reality that I only have two years left before he leaves for college, which triggers my anxiety, causing me to make a mental checklist of all the things he needs to know before he goes out on his own, and that's what keeps me up the rest of the night.

Sitting down for dinner a few weeks later, Sean is grinning sheepishly as he looks from me to David. "So, I was thinking. Now that I have my restricted license, can I drive myself to school this year?"

He's had his restricted license for a month now and other than a few short trips to the grocery store or a ride over to Noah or John's house, he hasn't driven much on his own.

David and I had been talking about the car situation and had already decided we would give Sean my car and I'd get a new one, so he asks Sean if he is absolutely, one-hundred percent sure he is ready to drive himself to and from school every day, to which Sean immediately replies "yes."

David looks at me and then turns to Sean. "Let's do this. Over the weekend Mom and I will go look at cars and you can use her car when we find a new one. We trust you and know you've been careful, but it's extremely important that you pay attention to your blood sugar when you get behind the wheel. You also have to agree that we all connect on the Find My Friends App."

Sean nods along as David lays out his rules.

"Thanks so much, you guys!" He's ecstatic, talking up a storm throughout dinner.

David and I purchase a new car on Saturday. By Tuesday, we've given Sean the keys to my old car, and he takes off immediately to spend his last days of summer with John and Noah. Toward the end of the week, Sean comes home and tells us some kids from school are getting together Saturday night to "kick off the school year" before classes start on Monday. John and Noah are going, and he asks if he could go too. I'm not excited about the kid hosting the party but I know Sean, and trusting he won't do anything too stupid, we tell him he can go. Because his license is restricted and he can't drive alone at night, I agree to drop him off and David will pick him up.

We plan to have dinner with Abby and Frank while the boys are at the party, agreeing to meet at a locally owned Mexican restaurant. When we pull up to drop Sean off, I'm shocked by the number of kids pouring into the house. Did they invite the entire class? I feel a little on edge when Sean gets out of the car. I remind him about sending a thumbs-up if his CGM alarms him and tell him to text David when he is ready is to be picked up. "I've got this, Mom. Stop worrying." He waves as he walks up the driveway with some of his classmates.

As soon as we sit down in the restaurant Abby leans over to me and whispers, "I have a bad feeling about this party. Do you think the parents are home? There were a lot of kids there."

"I'm not sure, but I have the same feeling. I hope everything goes ok."

Over dinner, David and Frank talk about planning another guys' trip with the boys, something involving the beach and lots of golf, with Abby and I encouraging them to make it happen. And then, an hour into our dinner, my phone vibrates. When I see it's Sean, I immediately answer. "Hey, is everything ok?"

"Mom, can you come get me and Noah?"

"Sure, I'm on my way right now. Are you ok?"

"Yes, we just want to leave."

"I'll be right there."

I hang up and grab my purse. "Sean and Noah want to be picked up. David and I will get them and meet you guys at your house." David stands up, throws some money on the table to cover our half of the bill and we rush out of the restaurant.

When we get to the party house, we notice a few police cars on the street. It's nearly impossible to find parking, but eventually we find a spot a few blocks away. As we walk toward the house, we see Sean and Noah sitting on the curb. There is a cop in the driveway, but he doesn't seem too concerned with our boys.

"What's going on?" David asks as we approach them.

"It was a disaster." Noah tells us. "The house was

packed, the music was so loud you couldn't talk and there were kegs of beer in every room. We were hanging out in the backyard when we heard the sirens and the next thing we knew, the cops were in the house breaking up the party."

"Were you drinking?" David asks.

"No, we weren't." Sean responds. "We were sitting by the pool talking with a few girls. When the cops came, they walked outside and asked to check our cups, then they told us to call our parents to pick us up and wait out front. They said a neighbor called and complained about the noise and that's what brought them here."

"Where's John?" I look from Sean to Noah, who are looking at each other.

Sean hesitates, then says, "He was inside the house when the cops came."

"Where is he now?" I ask, my voice impatient and rising as I look around the yard for John.

The boys eye each other again and then Noah looks at me and says, "He was drinking. The cops made him wait inside for his parents."

I close my eyes and take a deep breath. "Ok, let's go. Noah, your parents are waiting for us at your house."

I had texted Abby to say all was ok and we'd be there shortly, so I am not surprised to see her and Frank waiting on the porch when we pull into the driveway.

Noah fills them in on what happened, and more

details start coming out about how much everyone was drinking, including John, who had joined right in. Apparently, the guys had a slight falling out when John started to put some pressure on them to drink with him. After we exhaust the topic, the boys go inside to get a snack.

Abby turns to me with a look of genuine concern. "Have you heard from Valerie?"

"No. I'm sure she's beside herself, trying to deal with both John and Mike. I just hope John is ok and Mike doesn't find a way to blame her for this, too." I regret that last part as soon as it leaves my mouth, but my disdain for how Mike treats Valerie is getting harder to hide. Not surprisingly, Abby agrees with me.

Monday morning, Sean is up early and ready for his first day of junior year. I ask him to double-check his backpack to make sure he has everything he needs, and remind him that after work I'll be at the school for a Parent Org. meeting and offer to drop off his backup supplies at the nurse's office, which he appreciates.

I walk him to the car and watch as he puts his backpack on the passenger seat and then walks around to the driver's side. When I remind him to take his time and drive safely, he tilts his head, smirks, and then says, "I've got this, Mom." He gives me a hug and gets in the car, leaving me alone on the driveway watching him pull out of our cul-de-sac. When did my baby grow up? Time is moving a little too fast for me. I shake my head as I go back inside to get a cup of coffee.

Just then, my phone dings with a text message from Abby. "Noah just drove off in my old car, which is now his new car. YIKES!"

I text back right away. "Sean too! Have you heard anything from Valerie yet?"

"Nothing. You?"

I call her because it's too much to text.

As soon as she answers I say, "Nothing. I have a Breakthrough T1D meeting tomorrow morning. I'm hoping she'll be there. I'm worried about her and John."

"I am too. Noah hasn't heard from John, but I'm sure they'll smooth things over today. They have several classes together."

"I hope so. Sean didn't hear from him either. I have to run, but I'll let you know if I hear from Valerie."

But I hear nothing from her all day. I send her several texts and leave a message, but get no response, which is highly unusual.

I'm eager for Sean to come home from school, so when he finally walks through the door, I'm waiting for him. When I ask how his day was, he tells me it was great. He's happy with his teachers, dodged a bullet for English in not getting Mrs. Carey, who has a reputation for being mean, and is relieved to have a few classes with Noah. He's grabbing a snack out of the pantry, putting his carbs in his pump at the same time. I'm hungry for information about John, so I ask if they have any classes together and if they've spoken since Saturday.

His response is clipped and to the point. "He's in my English class. We sat next to each other, but he didn't have much to say. At lunch he sat with some of the kids from lacrosse."

After he goes to his room, I try Valerie one more time, but the call instantly goes to voicemail, and this time, I don't bother leaving a message.

Fifty

Tuesday morning, when I arrive for the outreach meeting, Hope is already sitting with a few of the other volunteers I've gotten to know over the past several months, but Valerie is nowhere to be found. We stall as long as we can to give her a chance to arrive, but when she doesn't, we move forward and I watch the clock, praying she will walk through the door. But she never does.

Following the meeting, as everyone gets up to leave, Hope asks me to stay behind. In her office, I take a seat in front of her desk, and she informs me that Naomi Smith has agreed to chair the gala this year, which I think is wonderful. I liked Naomi the minute I met her two years ago, after her daughter was diagnosed with T1D. After Hope invites me to lunch with her and Naomi and we agree on the following Thursday, I enter the details in my calendar and gather my things to leave.

As soon as I get in my car, I try calling Valerie. I was shocked she wasn't at the meeting and now I'm really concerned when my call, once again, goes directly to voicemail. I send a text message that I am on my way over and, after picking up a drive-thru coffee, I head straight to her house.

When I get there, the front door is open, so I knock and walk inside. Valerie comes to the door in yoga pants and a wrinkled T-shirt. Her hair is a mess, her eyes are swollen and red from crying and she looks like she hasn't slept in days. When I hand her a cup of coffee, she looks sad when she comments, "You always know exactly what I need."

"So, I guess you heard what happened Saturday night?" she asks, between sips, sounding so defeated as I follow her into the family room, where we settle on her couch.

"I know about the party and the police because Sean and Noah were there, and I had to go pick them up. Is John ok?"

"Other than the fact that he's grounded for the next month, I guess he's ok. He was pretty drunk when we got there. Mike went inside to get him, because, according to him, I'm not capable of handling the situation rationally. Luckily, the police basically gave John a warning and said if they catch him drinking at another party, they'll arrest him for underage drinking. I think they also gave the owners of the house a warning that if they allow a party like that at their house again, they will be arrested."

I'm not sure what to say, so I simply rub her back and wait for her to continue.

"There was so much fallout from the weekend I don't even know how to process it all. You know, I understand the experimenting and wanting to fit in with the cool kids. But I thought having T1D would make him a little more cautious. He fell asleep the minute we got home, and I sat up the entire night watching his blood sugar in case he crashed. My biggest fear with drinking is that he will have a low blood sugar and not wake up. And he didn't even have any remorse the next morning. When Mike told him he was grounded and the only time he would be leaving the house for the next month was for school, he just stared at him and said 'ok.' He has a therapy appointment this week and I can't decide if I should give the therapist a heads-up about the party or let him work it out for himself."

Not sure how to respond, I ask, "What does Mike say?"

"Nothing. He says nothing. He doesn't want to talk about it. As far as he's concerned, John is fine and he's living with the consequences."

"Then maybe you let it go. Chalk it up to things teens do and move on."

"Thank you for not judging me or John. It means a lot."

"Valerie, you know me better than that. Drinking at a party doesn't make John a bad kid. It makes him a typical teenager who made a mistake."

I start to rise from the couch when Valerie reaches out and pulls me back down, then proceeds to burst into tears. The flood gates are wide open, so I grab a box of tissues, giving her time to collect herself. Between sobs she blurts out, "Mike left."

I shake my head and stare at her, wondering if I heard her correctly, when she tells me that the day after the party, Mike came into the kitchen holding a duffle bag and asked her to follow him into his office. "He basically said he can't take living this way anymore, that this is not the life he signed up for, and that he doesn't recognize me anymore. Apparently, I'm no longer the fun-loving, easygoing, carefree, spirited woman he married. At first, I tried to convince him that we could work it out, possibly see a marriage counselor, or spend more time together doing the things we used to both enjoy, but his answer was a hard no. And then it dawned on me that he must have been thinking about this for quite some time, because the final blow was that he had already rented an apartment."

At a complete loss for words, I stare at her, handing her tissue after tissue as she wipes her eyes, which are still overflowing. My thoughts turn to John. This poor kid has so much on his plate already, and now he's got to deal with this. When I ask how he took the news, Valerie says he was fine, almost relieved that maybe now the fighting will stop, but she's not sure it's really hit him yet.

Fifty-one

On Friday afternoon, Sean comes home from school exhausted. I'm carrying his laundry basket through the room where he is lying on the couch watching TV when he stops me. A classmate, James Peterman, has invited Sean and some other friends, including Noah and some of the basketball players, to go bowling to celebrate James's birthday. Nonchalantly, I ask if John was invited and find myself a little disappointed when Sean says no.

The following night, a few hours after Sean leaves for the party, he calls to ask if he can spend the night at James's house. A few of the guys are staying and they plan on watching movies and hanging out. "Sure," I tell him. "Text me in the morning and I'll come pick you up."

David and I fall asleep early, but at three o'clock my phone alarms, letting me know that Sean is going low. As a matter of fact, the word LOW is in all caps, which means he is below thirty. I text him and get no response. I call him and it rings five times before going to voicemail. I try again and again and get the same results. David is now trying to reach Noah, who also stayed overnight, but is having no luck. I'm starting to panic, so I get the school directory and look up the Peterman's phone number. His mom, Sally, answers on the second ring and I apologize for waking her. I tell her about Sean and she takes the phone with her to the boys' room, wakes Sean and hands him the phone. He tells me he didn't get an alert but looks at his app and sees LOW. He tests his blood sugar and it's 126. He must have slept on it which sometimes causes a compression low.

"Oh my God, Mom, why did you call Mrs. Peterman?"

"Because I tried calling you several times and you didn't answer. We tried Noah's phone and he didn't answer either."

"I'm fine. My number is fine. If I was low, I would have woken up. This is so embarrassing."

"Sean, we can discuss this in the morning. For now, make sure your sound is on because I tried calling you several times and you never answered."

"I'm hanging up." He disconnects the call, and I am livid. Not only was I scared to death when I saw LOW displayed, but then not being able to reach him gave me time to imagine all sorts of horrific scenarios. How dare he get mad at me for being concerned about him?

The next morning, Sean texts me to say they are ready to be picked up. After David goes to get them and drops Noah off, they arrive home. Sean stomps through the door and heads directly toward his room.

"Wait just a second," I say, so sternly that he abruptly

turns around. He looks at me like he's about to argue, but I don't give him the chance. "Sit down right now."

He can tell by the tone of my voice that I'm not playing around, so he immediately puts his backpack down and sits on the couch.

"Last night when we got that alarm and couldn't reach you, we were frightened. Use your imagination and put yourself in our shoes for just a minute. We had no idea if you were awake, asleep, or unconscious. All we knew was your blood sugar was reading as LOW, not even a number, but LOW, and we couldn't reach you. What choices did we have? How would you have wanted us to react at that point?"

He sinks back into the couch, looks at me for a minute and then shrugs. "I understand why you called Mrs. Peterman. I just wish you hadn't. I was so embarrassed that my friend's mother had to wake me, and I wasn't even low."

"I understand that. And I'm sorry you were embarrassed. But we had no way to know if you were low or not based on the information we had from the app, so we had to take action. Look, Sean, we trust you completely. We know you're responsible and can take care of yourself. But this is new territory for us, and we're going to make mistakes. We'd never do anything to intentionally hurt or embarrass you. At the same time, your safety is our number one priority."

David interjects and says, "Let's do this. Put our numbers on emergency bypass. This way, even if your sound is off it will ring if we call you. We'll do the same with your number so you can always reach us. Does that sound agreeable to you?"

Sean nods and takes out his phone to make the adjustment. "Can I go now? I want to take a shower."

I nod, and as he picks up his backpack on his way to his room, I call after him sternly, "And one last thing. Don't you ever hang up on me again."

Fifty-two

After several weeks of trying to coordinate our schedules, I'm finally meeting Sherry for lunch at City Block Burgers. It's not our usual go-to place for lunch, but Sherry wanted to try it, so I agreed. After we order, we compare notes on our college tours and speculate where our boys will ultimately attend school. I'm dying to ask if Billy is still close with Cory but decide against it. Since David and I occasionally attend Friday night services at the synagogue, I'm slowly repairing my relationship with God and as an added bonus, I've reconnected with old friends, grateful that we never run into Karen or her family. We talk a little bit about the gala and I'm pleasantly surprised when Sherry tells me she spoke with Hope and has decided to join the committee this year. For the last few years, she and Richard have attended as our guests so I'm glad she's getting more involved.

Following lunch, I stop by Abby's house. She is starting a kitchen renovation, so I help her empty her cabinets and we catch up on the school gossip. We talk a little about Valerie, mostly how worried we are about her. We've both been reaching out, inviting her to join us on several occasions, but she always declines, saying she needs time to adjust to her "new normal."

When I ask Abby if Noah mentions John at all, she says no. She thinks Noah is still hurt by the way John acted at the party, and while he cares about John, he doesn't want to hang out with John's new friends. It makes me a little sad to see a rift between the boys, since they have been such good friends for so long.

That night at dinner when Sean shares a few funny stories about kids at school, I take advantage of the opportunity and ask him how John is, but he shrugs his shoulders. He says John has been distant lately and spends most of his time with a group of guys from lacrosse. Then, completely out of left field, he tells us that Saturday night he and Noah are taking two of the girls from their class to the movies. David and I look at each other with raised eyebrows. Apparently, Noah is interested in Brooke, who is a cheerleader, and Sean's date is Sydney, a girl he works with on the yearbook committee. David and I are hitting each other under the table as Sean leaves the room. "Oh my God! Our little boy has a date!" I giggle as I clear the plates, while David puffs out his chest and says, "That's my boy."

Later in the week, I'm volunteering at the school bookstore when John walks in with one of his new friends and we chat a little bit. He appears to be doing okay, and his friend is polite and friendly when John introduces us. Even if our boys drift apart, I'm as close as ever with Valerie and will always consider John family. As I'm leaving the school, I almost collide with Garrett as he comes barreling out of his office. Stopping just short of knocking me over, he seizes the opportunity to let me know he reached out to Mrs. Lacky, who will be filing the necessary documentation to arrange for accommodations during standardized testing on Sean's behalf. We chat briefly about what's involved and as I make my way to the car, I get a little teary-eyed. I knew junior year was going to be intense, but I didn't anticipate feeling so emotional every time we mentioned the word college.

Straight from school, I drive to the restaurant to meet Hope and Naomi for lunch. The hostess leads me to the table where they are already seated, and I'm shocked to see David with them. I slide into the booth next to him, facing Naomi and Hope.

Kissing him on the cheek, I say, "Hey, you! I didn't know you were joining us for lunch."

He gives me a sideways hug. "Surprise!"

Hope takes control of the conversation, and after a few minutes of the requisite chit-chat, she takes out a folder marked GALA.

"Okay friends, let's get down to business before our food comes." She holds her hands out, palms up, toward Naomi and asks, "Would you like to do the honors?"

Naomi nods and turns toward me. "Jessie, you have

done so much for the T1D community since Sean was diagnosed. You have led walk teams, worked on the walk committee, you've been an advocate and a mentor, not to mention the many times you've chaired the gala. All that to say, Jessie, we want to honor you at this year's gala."

I stare at her and then look from her to Hope to David, who is beaming with pride.

"I don't know what to say. I'm at a loss for words."

"Yes would be a great word!" says Hope.

I look to David. "Did you know about this?"

"I just found out yesterday. When Naomi called me, I couldn't think of a better, more deserving person for them to honor."

Naomi leans across the table and takes my hand. "So, what do you say?"

"I say YES! Thank you so much for the honor."

The next hour is spent on details about the gala and what my role as honoree entails. David offers a few suggestions for potential sponsors and Naomi shares with me her vision for the evening. I'm in shock and can't wait to tell Sean. It's going to be hard keeping this from Abby and Valerie, but Naomi asks me to hold off telling my friends, as they would like to make an official announcement. In the parking lot, I hug Hope and Naomi and lean against the car, talking to David as they drive off.

"David, this feels so surreal. I mean, what did I really do to deserve this?"

"Are you kidding me? Since the moment Sean was diagnosed you've been on a mission. I'm just so happy they recognize all the work you've done. I'm so proud of you." He kisses me and we agree to wait for dinner to tell Sean together.

Later that night at the dinner table, David taps his glass with the side of his knife. "We have a big announcement tonight." Sean looks from David to me and back to David, who is pausing for dramatic effect. He lifts his glass and says "Cheers to you, Jessie. The Breakthrough T1D Gala Honoree." Sean smiles and pumps his fist in the air. He jumps up from his seat to hug me, and we share with him the very few details we have so far. Once we exhaust the topic, Sean fills us in on his day, entertaining us with a story from lunch that included Noah, Brooke, and Sydney. I ask him when we get to meet these girls, and he smiles shyly and says "Soon."

On date night, Sean takes forever getting ready. When he finally comes out of his room, he's wearing khaki pants and a tucked-in button-down shirt, causing me to do a double take. "Where are your gym shorts?" I tease him as he grabs his test kit and a tube of glucose tablets to put in his backpack.

"Haha. Very funny, Mom. Noah will be here in a few minutes to pick me up." Now that Noah is seventeen, his license is unrestricted so he can drive at night.

Impulsively, I give him a hug and tell him how much

I love him. "I hope you have a great time tonight. Please text me when you're on your way home."

"I will." I hear the horn beep, and Sean heads out the door.

After he leaves, David and I pick up Valerie, finally convincing her that she is not a "third wheel," as she refers to herself, on our way to meet Abby and Frank for dinner. Thirty minutes into our evening, I notice Karen and Jerry being escorted by the hostess to a table and recognize the couple joining them from the synagogue. The other couple notices us and waves, prompting us to wave back, and before it even registers with me, David excuses himself and walks over to say hello. I stay with my friends, having no desire to talk to Karen. As I watch him make small talk with the two men, I instinctively tense up, but Abby reaches under the table and squeezes my leg, which diverts my attention, and I am grateful that she and Valerie know the entire Karen saga and always have my back.

On our way home I get a text from Sean. "I've got my number. Also, we are going to hang out at Sydney's house for a little while. And yes, her parents are home." The message is followed by a laughing emoji. I give him a thumbs-up and then look at his CGM app. It's reading sixty-five so I relax and put down the phone. When I ask David about his conversation with Jerry, he says it was nothing special, but he hadn't seen him in so long he wanted to say hello. He doesn't believe he should hold Jerry accountable for his wife's rudeness. I disagree, pointing out that if I was rude and hurtful to a good friend, David would totally call me out on it, but I don't want to argue with him, so I let it go.

We get comfortable in the family room, eager for Sean to come home so we can hear about his night, and finally, we hear the garage door open and he joins us, full of energy and excitement. The movie was great. The company was better. "Oh, and by the way, I invited them all over to hang out tomorrow," he says, practically skipping out of the room.

The next morning, I witness a side of Sean I haven't seen before, as he straightens up the family room, cleans his bedroom and checks himself in the mirror more times than I can count. We're chatting with Noah when the doorbell rings. Sean yells, "I've got it," as he races to the door. After introducing us to Brooke, who is petite, blond and perky, everything you would expect from a cheerleader, he turns to Sydney and I can't help but notice how he gently touches her back as he says, "This is Sydney." Sydney is also petite, with light brown hair and big brown eyes, and a smile that lights up her face — I immediately see why Sean is taken with her. The girls chat with us a few minutes and then they all go upstairs to the rec room, where, a few hours later, I bring them snacks and invite them all to stay for dinner. After texting their parents, they are all in, so David runs to the store to pick up burgers and buns, and over the course of the evening they amuse us with stories about school and some of their friends. Since they are all juniors, we talk a little about the colleges they are looking into and what they want to study. After we clean up and they all leave, Sean thanks us for having them over, then goes inside to finish his homework and get ready for school the next day. I glance over at David, who has a glazed look on his face.

"Are you ok?" I ask him.

"I'm just wondering when he grew up." My sentiments exactly.

Fifty-three

Time passes way too quickly. Hope makes the announcement at a gala meeting about my honor and Valerie and Abby cheer for me as Sherry walks over to give me a hug. Relief washes over me, knowing I can finally share this with them, as it was so hard keeping this a secret from my closest friends. Sean is spending a lot of time with Sydney and Noah and Brooke seem to be an item as well. The four of them have fallen into a routine, spending Saturday nights together and on Sundays, Sydney joins us for dinner. We celebrate Sean's seventeenth birthday with an upgraded CGM courtesy of Peds Endo office and a little party for his friends, courtesy of me and David. By December, we feel as if Sydney is part of the family. Her mom Grace and I talk occasionally to keep up with the kids, and while I don't know her very well, we've been acquaintances through our volunteer work at the school. Sean has opted out of basketball this year, freeing up his time for other activities.

Over the holidays, I invite Abby and Valerie to celebrate Hanukkah with us, along with Sydney and Brooke. I offered for John to bring a friend, but Valerie said he would be joining us solo. Our kitchen counter overflows with homemade latkes, a brisket with a noodle kugel, along with jelly donuts and fruit for dessert. My heart is so full watching the kids all get along and listening to the laughter emanate from the family room.

Once we get through the holidays, life starts moving at lightning speed. Sean is busy with school, studying for the SAT's, and working on the yearbook. He asks Sydney to prom with a prom-posal that is so creative. He had decorated a poster with Polaroid pictures of the two of them doing different activities together, on the top of which he'd written, "Next on our bucket list: Dancing at Prom. Will you be my date?" Then he'd picked up four of her favorite cupcakes, each one with a letter on the top so when placed together, they spelled PROM. He told me that when she answered the door, she'd squealed and yelled "YES" before he could even ask. Later that day, Grace calls me to tell me how excited Sydney is. Prom is the week after gala, so we make sure to order Sean's tux early, but I nearly forget to order Sydney's corsage. If it weren't for Abby telling me she was about to order one for Brooke, I think I would have forgotten. I meet her at the florist, and we pick them out together.

Sean's standardized testing accommodations are approved, so he schedules his first SAT for a Saturday in February. Everything goes smoothly, although he tells me he had to take a break to eat so he wouldn't go low, but the proctor was very understanding. We meet with Garrett and Sean mentions he would like to look at the University of Miami, so we arrange for a tour over spring break, which is just a few weeks before gala. One of the perks of being the honoree is not having to worry about a lot of the small details, so I am able to plan our trip with very little stress.

The first Saturday of March, we fly into Miami and drive to Coral Gables. Our tour is scheduled for Monday, so we enjoy the weekend exploring the area. The tour is very impressive. The campus is beautiful, and Sean is really excited by everything they have to offer. After the tour, we drive to Key Largo, where we've rented a condo facing the ocean. I feel a twinge of sadness packing to go home, since it was such a fun week, and I loved having Sean and David all to myself.

With one week left until the gala, I start working on my speech. Now that it's a reality, I'm overwhelmed, feeling uncomfortable being singled out when so many people work so hard for this cause. I start and stop, then start again, writing and deleting until I finally find a groove. But then, I'm interrupted by the CGM alert on my phone. I glance over to see Sean's number is really high. I'm about to text him when he messages me to say he's aware and not sure what the problem is because he hasn't eaten since breakfast. I ask him if he is feeling ok and he assures me he is not sick, so we agree to give it an hour to see if it comes down. I'm watching the clock and trying not to look at the app too often, which, like watching water boil, never seems to change as quickly when you're looking. An hour passes and I check again and see he is still high. He calls and I pick up immediately.

"Hi, honey. What's going on?"

"I'm not sure. I just put this pod on last night. I think the cannula may have dislodged or it's a bad site because there's some blood on the adhesive. Can you bring me a new pod? I used my last one in the nurse's office a while ago and forgot to replace it."

I save my document, grab a few pods so I can leave some at school and head out the door. When I get there, I text him and he meets me in the nurse's office. He changes his pod, and I offer to drive him home, suggesting we could pick up his car later, but he says he can't miss class and will be ok. I can tell he's not feeling great from being so high He looks flushed and he's a bit agitated, but I know better than to argue with him in this state, so I give him a hug and tell him to call if he needs anything. Because I don't want to drive all the way home and turn around if he needs me, I sit in my car for an hour and watch his app. Finally, the arrow turns around and his number starts heading back down, so I drive home.

Later that night, we are eating dinner when his pod starts alarming. It makes that horrible screeching noise we've heard before and when he checks his pump it tells him the pod has failed. So, for the second time that day, Sean has to change his site, and we lose a reservoir full of insulin. Knowing he is due for a CGM sensor change, he does that at the same time. Unfortunately, it takes two hours for the sensor to warm up, so for now he will check his blood sugar the old-fashioned way and stick his finger. After dinner I call the 24-hour helpline and report both pods and they offer to replace them but they can't do anything about the insulin we lost.

Alone in our room, as we get ready for bed, I vent to David. "We need a cure. The technology is great and yes, we've come a long way since he was first diagnosed, but it's only great when it works. I don't even know how he functions half the time. Between the night alarms and the interruptions in class and the highs and lows, he has to be exhausted. And the most frustrating part is, if you didn't know he has T1D, looking at him, he appears healthy and vibrant. No one has any idea how hard he works to accomplish what he does."

Tears are streaming down my face now. David wraps his arms around me and lets me cry.

"And another thing," I continue, "How am I going to sleep when he is away at college?"

"Jessie, we have raised him to be independent and confident in his ability to manage life, including his diabetes. And just like when he is at school or at a friend's house, we are only a phone call away. We'll still be here to support him. He's got this. And when the time comes, we will get through it together."

"I know you're right; I just worry that he will get burnt out or that it will become overwhelming for him. I'm still angry sometimes. Not a 'why me?' but 'why anyone?' Why can't we fix this?"

Fifty-four

My *stomach is in knots* from a mix of excitement and anticipation on the day of the gala. I'm not a fan of being front and center, and the thought of giving a speech in front of 400 guests is giving me major stage fright. But then I glance over at a picture of Sean that hangs on our wall. It's the one we took in Hilton Head right before he was diagnosed. His face is tilted toward the sun with the most beautiful smile, and he seems not to have a care in the world, with no idea how his world is about to change. It fuels me. He has had to push through so many obstacles, and he does it so gracefully. If he can face all these challenges with such a great attitude, then I have no excuse not to push myself out of my comfort zone. I practice my speech one more time and put it away.

Sydney is joining us tonight and, since I offered to treat, we are meeting at the salon for a mani-pedi and a blowout. I extended the invitation to Valerie and Abby too, but they are busy setting up for tonight. Sherry bought two tables this year and filled them with friends from the synagogue. I snuck a look at her guest list, relieved to see that Karen and Jerry were not attending.

Not that I thought they would, but Karen and Sherry are still very close friends.

Sydney is so sweet, and she adores Sean. We have such a lovely afternoon together talking about *The Bachelor*, and I now know way more about The Kardashians than I ever wanted to know, but I enjoy her take on the shows and am happy to have some girl time. When I get home from the salon, I finish my makeup and slide on my gown. Sean and David are waiting for me in the family room, and as I enter, David starts to whistle and Sean says, "Wow, Mom, you look great."

"Thanks, honey. You both look so handsome. Sean, Sydney is going to flip when she sees you."

Sean blushes and that's when I hear someone clear their throat. When I turn to look in the hallway, my mouth drops open and tears pool in my eyes. Standing there in their formal attire are my mom and dad. Before I can say anything, my mom has her arms around me, holding on tight and says, "I'm so proud of you." Then she passes me to my dad.

When I turn back to David, his arms are wide open as he exclaims, "Surprise!"

David grabs his house keys as I double-check my purse to make sure I have my speech, and as we walk out the door, I take a deep breath. Then I do a double-take when I see a limousine waiting in our driveway to take us all to the gala, a very extravagant and out-of-character splurge for David that I never saw coming. This night just keeps getting better. We make one stop to pick up Sydney, who looks stunning, and we are on our way.

It's a whirlwind of activity when we arrive. We take pictures on the "red carpet" as a family and then Sean and Sydney take one together and David and I do as well. We don't make it far into the cocktail area before we are stopped by various guests and volunteers we've gotten to know through the years. Across the room, my eyes lock with Valerie's, so I grab David's hand, and we weave through the crowd to catch up to her. Abby and Frank join us and, since they remember meeting my parents at Sean's bar mitzvah, they greet each other warmly, and we all chat until the ballroom doors open, and we are invited to take our seats. Our table is front and center and to the right of us is Valerie's table, where Abby and Frank are sitting tonight, and behind our table are Sherry's two tables. I stop on my way to say hello to everyone from the synagogue and when I hug Sherry I say in her ear, "Thank you so much for bringing them all tonight."

She hugs me back and says, "I'm very proud of you, my friend."

Sean comes over with Sydney to say hello to Sherry and then we all take our seats. The emcee welcomes everyone and then introduces Naomi, who shares a little of her daughter's story and then gives everyone an overview of the evening's agenda. After she steps away, the emcee takes over and thanks all the gala sponsors by name, finally reminding everyone the silent auction is still open, and the program will begin after dinner.

Forty-five minutes later the emcee is back on the stage. Plates are being cleared, and we are ready to get started. The silent auction is now closing, so the emcee leads the crowd in a countdown and the silent auction is officially closed. I haven't seen the agenda, and I have no idea who is introducing me, so I am so touched when the emcee invites Valerie to the stage.

"Good evening, everyone. Several years ago, I received a call from a very scared, tired mom whose son had just been diagnosed with T1D. Little did I know, when I agreed to meet her for coffee, that not only would Jessie Greene become one of my best friends, but she would become *my* rock and support along this crazy journey with type 1 diabetes. Jessie, you are the epitome of making lemonade out of lemons. I am so honored and grateful to know you and call you my chosen sister."

The audience applauds and Valerie holds up her hands. "Please welcome Jessie's husband, David." He gives my hand a squeeze as he gets up and walks to the stage.

"Good evening. Thank you all for being here tonight and honoring my wife, Jessie. Within a few months of Sean being diagnosed, Jessie was introduced to Valerie, who in turn, introduced us to Breakthrough T1D. Once we learned about the organization, we were all in. Typical of Jessie, she has thrown her heart and soul into doing everything she can to advance Breakthrough T1D's mission, and while I won't list every detail of her commitment to this organization, I will acknowledge she has chaired this gala more times than I can remember. But above and beyond all else, she has been an incredible mom and caregiver to our son Sean. Jessie, I am so proud of you, and I love you with all my heart." Everyone is clapping and I'm about to stand up when I feel a hand on my shoulder. Hope kneels down next to me and says, "Not yet." The room goes dark, and Sean's face appears on the big screens flanking the stage.

"Hi, Mom. I just want to say thank you. You work tirelessly trying to cure T1D and I know you do that for me. No matter how busy you are, you always put me first. You are there whenever I need you, even if it's at three o'clock in the morning. I can't tell you how much it means to me. I love you so much."

I'm wiping the tears away when the lights come back on, and Hope leads me to the stage.

The emcee approaches the microphone and says, "Ladies and Gentleman, please welcome our Gala Honoree, Jessie Greene." Everyone is on their feet applauding as I approach the podium. I look out over the crowd, seeking out Valerie and Abby, my closest friends, then shift my sight to Sherry's tables and the people who have known us since Sean was a baby. My gaze lingers on my husband and son standing next to each other clapping, and then to my mom and dad, who traveled to be with us tonight. I'm overwhelmed with love. The room quiets down, and everyone takes their seats as I place my speech on the podium. I take a deep breath and begin.

"Thank you to Hope, Naomi and the gala committee for this extraordinary honor. I am extremely humbled. The summer our son Sean was diagnosed with type 1 diabetes, as many of you will understand, we were devastated. We knew nothing about type 1 diabetes, nor did we know anyone who had it. In the hospital on that dreadful day, we made a promise to Sean. 'We will do everything within our power to help you. And we won't stop until there is a cure.'

"Shortly after Sean was diagnosed, I called Denise at the Peds Endo office and asked if she could put me in touch with someone who had a son Sean's age. I knew enough in that moment to realize we needed support, and I had to do something, not only for David and me, but especially for Sean. Meeting Valerie, becoming sisters-in-arms, not only helped us through a difficult adjustment, but it also gave me the gift of a forever friend.

"When Valerie invited us to participate in our first Breakthrough T1D Walk, we were unsure what to expect. I'll never forget the feeling I had arriving at the park that day. Seeing how many families were there and noticing all those kids wearing insulin pumps brought me to tears. That day, I knew then that we were not alone. The T1D community is small but it is fierce. We support each other through the challenges. We can vent to each other and understand without having to explain. Living with a life-threatening, chronic disease or caring for a person, especially a child with a chronic disease, can be extremely isolating. In our community, we take care of each other.

"Yes, I have worked hard over the last nine years, but my involvement with this community has given me so much in return. Let's be honest. As caregivers, there is not much we can do for our T1Ds. We can offer support by filling their insulin pumps or giving them their shots. We can order their supplies and sit with them when their blood sugar is out of control...but what can we really do to fix it? For our family, when we leave a Breakthrough T1D function, we feel a sense of accomplishment. We did something that made a difference in Sean's life. We gave him hope. We reminded him we are doing everything we can to ensure his future is safer and healthier.

"These last several years have been life-changing in so many ways. Like all of you in this room today, we made a choice to act. We did not sit back and wait. We will continue to work hard, and we will keep pushing this needle forward, so when the day comes and this disease is cured, we will take pride in knowing that we had a hand in making that happen.

"I want to thank our family and friends, who not only support us emotionally, but also contribute to our fundraising efforts. It's hard to ask for help and you have been here every step of the way.

"My darling David. I love you with all my heart. You are an amazing partner, husband and best friend, but above all else, you are an incredible father and Sean hit the jackpot with you as his dad. Sean, you are the greatest gift I've ever received. There are no words to truly express my pride and admiration for you. You weren't handed an easy road, but you walk it with grace and dignity. I love you more than you will ever know. You are both the loves of my life. Together we are a small but mighty team. Sean, I hope you always know that Dad and I will never break our promise to you. The one we made that very first day when you were diagnosed. We won't stop until there's a cure. You can't quit, so we won't quit."

Tears are streaming down my face as David and Sean join me on the stage, and we embrace each other, then together, we return to our seats. The rest of the evening is a blur. When they announce the total for the evening, we are blown away. My heart is full of love and gratitude for each person in that room because I truly believe they are making a difference, and one day we will come together to celebrate a cure. At the after-party, Sherry grabs me and pulls me onto the dance floor along with Valerie and Abby. If you had told me nine years ago that the four of us would be dancing together, I would have had a hard time believing it, but tonight I am just grateful.

Fifty-five

∞

Monday morning, it's business as usual. With junior year winding down, Sean's focus is on crafting his college essays, which Garrett encourages him to start writing now, since he plans on meeting with him over the summer to proofread them. David and I are surprised to learn that Sean has narrowed his list to three schools, and while he hasn't decided which is his number one yet, he appears to be partial to the marketing program at Miami. All applications must be submitted by mid-October to meet the deadline for early action, with decisions arriving by mid-to-late December. Garrett asks Sean to consider adding a few schools to his list, but Sean prefers to keep the list small. With his grades, test scores and extracurricular activities, he should easily qualify for them all. Interestingly, Noah is applying to the same schools, and they hope to go to college together, while John prefers to go to school on the West Coast. He is very interested in filmmaking and would like to get into the theatre program at UCLA or Southern Cal.

After work, I go to the gym and then run a few errands. I'm checking out at the grocery store when David calls, wanting to know if we have plans this weekend. A colleague of his has invited us to get together for dinner so I offer up Saturday night, reminding him that Friday is prom night, and we are having dinner with Abby and Valerie after the photo op. The entire junior class and their dates are meeting at the park to take pictures before they go to prom. I think I'm more excited than Sean.

Friday night, it's a challenge to find parking, but we finally find a spot and walk a few blocks to the park entrance. I'm watching the kids arrive, recognizing most of them from my time in the bookstore. They all say hello as the file past us to the designated picture-taking area that has been decorated with balloons. We are standing with Abby, Frank and Valerie when finally, Noah and Brooke arrive, followed by Sean and Sydney and John with his date. The girls look gorgeous, and I hug Sydney and tell her just how beautiful she is.

It's a bit chaotic as one of the prom moms is calling for all the guys to gather for a picture in front of the balloon arch. It's like herding cats, but finally they get them all together for a group picture. My heart soars to see John, Noah and Sean standing together with their arms around each other in the middle of the second row, and even though all the moms are jockeying for position because everyone wants the best angle possible, I manage to get a few great pictures of my own before prom mom calls for the girls. When it's finally time for them to leave for the prom, Sean comes over to give me a hug. I hold on a little tighter, recognizing that every milestone feels huge to me right now, and whisper in his ear, "Be safe, make good choices and have the best night ever. I love you."

He whispers back, "I'll be safe, I'll make good choices and I plan on having the best night ever. I love you too." He smiles, side hugs David and takes Sydney's hand as they leave the park. Grace has offered to host the after-party, so following prom, Sean will go back to Sydney's house, along with four other couples, where they will spend the night, and we won't see Sean until the morning.

I purposely don't mention a word about diabetes to Sean. I don't want to give it one second of attention on this special night. I saw him put some glucose tablets in his pocket and I know he left an overnight bag with extra supplies at Sydney's before they left for the park. I say a little prayer that diabetes behaves tonight, and that Sean can be as carefree as his friends.

David and I are holding hands and sharing our own prom memories on the way back to the car. At the restaurant, Valerie, Abby and I sit across from Frank and David and while they talk about golf and the Masters tournament, we talk about the girls' dresses and how handsome our boys looked. The conversation moves on to vacations and we start making a bucket list of all the places we want to see and things we want to do. The guys cut in on our conversation and I start to think some of those dream trips may happen once our boys are settled in college. Later that night I scroll through social media to look at all the pictures the moms are posting. I'm aware of the clock and watching my phone for a text from Sean. Finally, my phone dings with his message. "I'm at Sydney's house. Prom was awesome! Can't wait to tell you all about it tomorrow."

I text him back, then put down my phone and go to sleep. When I wake up and look at the clock, to my surprise, it's eight a.m. and I've slept through the entire night. I can't remember the last time that happened. David is in the kitchen making coffee and, after he hands me a mug, I take a sip and follow him to the table. He's made waffles with eggs and bacon for us. I lean over, kiss him, then immediately dig in, getting a little glimpse of what life will be like when we are empty nesters, and think I might like it.

Sean comes home in the afternoon, looking exhausted but so happy. He sits with us for a few minutes, sharing the highlights of prom, and then excuses himself to take a shower and a nap. Later in the day, he spends a few more minutes with us, then grabs his keys and says he is going to Noah's. They are taking the girls to a movie tonight. As he's walking out the door, I remind him we have plans with David's colleague that evening and to text me when he is on his way home. I have a sneaky suspicion this is what our summer is going to look like.

Fifty-six

∞

It turns out summer for Sean is a mixed bag of essay writing and deciding if he should take the SAT one more time. In the end, he decides he is happy with his scores and will focus on his writing. He spends a lot of time with Sydney, who is also working on her applications. They have such a good time together and I can't help but wonder where this will go when they leave for college. In July, we spend a relaxing week at the beach, but once we get home, I barely see Sean. His essays are finished and all that's left is for him to complete the admissions applications, so he spends most of his time with Sydney, Noah and Brooke. Occasionally he and Noah meet up with John, who seems to be doing much better this summer. From what Valerie tells me, John has adjusted to his parents' divorce and seems happier now that there is no tension in the house.

The weekend before the boys begin senior year, we host our final back-to-school cookout and I'm filled with joy to see John, Noah and Sean spending time together. Valerie, Abby, and I are sitting on my sun deck when they start discussing all the things the boys will need for college and express genuine shock when they learn that I haven't started thinking about it yet. We all know I'm a big planner, but my only plan for senior year is to be present and live in the moment. I'll be ready when the time comes, but for now, I just want to enjoy my days with Sean and David.

Monday morning, I stand in the driveway waving good-bye and feeling a little emotional as Sean leaves for his first day of senior year. Fortunately, I don't have too much time to dwell on it, as I must get to work. Valerie texts me later in the day asking if I have time to grab lunch tomorrow after the first Parent Organization meeting of the school year, to which I reply, "Absolutely!"

When I arrive at the school, I notice Valerie's on the phone, standing beside her car and looking frazzled.

"Are you ok?" I mouth as approach her.

"Yes. Good lunch story," she answers.

After the meeting, we meet at the Salad Factory. "Wait until you hear this one." Valerie begins, as she takes her seat. "Apparently John was thinking of asking Lindsay Sharpe out on a date. They've been texting and talking on the phone a lot and spending time together with a group of mutual friends. He mentioned it to his friend Danny, who thought it was a great idea. Then last night Danny calls John and tells him that he shouldn't ask Lindsay out. When John asks why, he says, "it's a problem with her mother.""

She pauses as the server brings our salads over. Once our meals are delivered, she continues.

"When John asked what the problem was, Danny said he wasn't completely sure, but he thought it had something to do with his diabetes. He suggested that John talk to Lindsay about it before asking her out."

"Are you kidding me?" I'm getting so mad I think I'm turning red.

"Well," Valerie says, "John was upset and called Lindsay. He came right out and told her he would like to take her on a date, and she said she'd been hoping he'd ask her out. He asked her point blank if his diabetes made her uncomfortable and she assured him it did not. They made plans for this past weekend and then the day before, she called him and canceled. I happened to be talking to my friend Stephanie, who is friends with Lindsay's mom, so I asked her if she knew if there was a problem. She told me that Lindsay's mom is friends with your old buddy Karen. Apparently, Karen told her that it wasn't safe for Lindsay to drive in a car with John because if he goes low, he could pass out and cause an accident."

Furiously, Valerie asks, barely keeping her voice down, "Where the hell does she get her information and what the hell is her problem?"

I place my hand on Valerie's arm and try to soothe her. She is so worked up now and honestly, I'm fuming. What is wrong with her? Anyone can get sick behind the wheel and John is extremely careful about driving. She is so ignorant I just want to scream.

"How is John?"

"He's confused. He doesn't know what Stephanie told me. He just thinks Lindsay changed her mind and he doesn't understand why, since they've been flirting for months now. I feel so bad for him. I remember when he started wearing his pump and CGM I worried that people would be put off because he wears two devices. Turns out his friends have been so supportive, and Lindsay is well aware of his diabetes, and it obviously doesn't bother her. So, do I get involved? Do I educate Lindsay's mom?"

"No, you can't get involved with Lindsay's mom. We hardly know her. I say we talk to Sherry and hold a little T1D education class for Karen."

"Do you really want to do that?"

"Yes. I've been angry ever since Sherry told me how Karen got in Sherry's head with all the reasons they shouldn't be alone with Sean. Sherry has a dog in this fight too. I'm sure she'd be furious if someone treated her niece this way. It's time Karen was set straight on what life with T1D is really like. I only pray she never learns firsthand because she'd be a horrible support system."

As soon as I get in the car, I call Sherry. I fill her in, and she is appalled, but when I share my idea about educating Karen, Sherry seem hesitant. "I'm not sure it will help. She is so set in her ways and thinks she knows everything about literally everything. That being said, I can try to arrange a time to get together to give you the opportunity to resolve this."

"I appreciate it, Sherry. I'm sorry to put you in the middle, but I know if I call her, she won't respond."

"No worries. If this happened to my niece or my son, I'd be upset too. I'll let you know when I reach her."

We hang up and I try to visualize how this conversation is going to play out. I know if we are going to get through to Karen, we must approach this logically and not let our emotions get the better of us.

A few days later Sherry calls to say she arranged lunch with Karen for the following Thursday and just like that, our plan is set in motion.

Thursday, I'm uneasy as I drive to the restaurant. I'm not a fan of confrontation so I try to look at this as education. Karen is about to get schooled on T1D. Valerie and I arrive early so we can be seated at our table when they arrive. We each order a salad but end up pushing our food around the plate, feeling much too nervous to eat. It's not long before Sherry and Karen arrive. Once I see the server take their order I nod to Valerie, and we get up. As we approach their table, Karen notices us and looks uncomfortable. All these years later, I can still read her expressions.

"Hi, ladies," I say, as I pull out one of the chairs.

Valerie sits across from me and says, "How are you both today?"

Sherry smiles and feigns surprise at seeing us. "Hi! We just ordered. Do you want to join us?"

"No thanks. We just ate." Valerie says. "But we'd love to visit for a few minutes. Gosh, Karen, it's been a long time."

Karen squirms in her seat. "It has been. How are you?"

"Actually, I'm not so great. It seems there are some misconceptions going around about my son and his ability to safely drive because of his diabetes." Valerie pauses for a minute in order to give Karen a chance to absorb what she just said. Karen looks down at her lap and then up at Valerie, who takes this as her cue to continue. She goes on to explain what type 1 diabetes is and then goes into detail about the technology John uses to manage his disease. Karen listens politely and I can't tell if the information is getting through to her, when Valerie wraps up her lecture by saying, "All of this to say, he is as safe driving as any of our kids. If anything, our boys are more aware of their health and know they have to take those additional steps to be safe."

Valerie pauses to let this all sink in, which gives Karen a chance to speak up.

"I feel a little ambushed here. What is all this about?" She looks from Valerie to me and settles on Sherry, who immediately steps in.

"Karen, you may think you mean well, but you have wrong-headed notions about type 1 diabetes, and since my niece was diagnosed, I've come to realize that most people who aren't closely affected by T1D don't understand it."

I see this as my opening and chime in. "Karen, when Sean was diagnosed, you pulled away from me. It was obvious you didn't want to be responsible for Sean if he was alone with you and you seemed to prefer he not spend as much time with Cory. At the time, I was in crisis mode and was consumed with learning how to help Sean, which didn't leave me the energy to deal with our issues. But the truth is, I was beyond hurt. If it were Cory, how would you feel? Would you want people to understand his condition, or would you rather they make assumptions and spread misinformation? Because right now, that's exactly what you're doing."

Valerie places her hand on Karen's arm. "Karen, to use your words, we didn't want to ambush you, but we knew if we reached out to you, you'd never make time for us to talk. I just want you to know that if you have questions or aren't sure about something T1D-related, you can ask us. But please stop encouraging other people to fear our boys."

Karen blinks back tears, and speaks so softly I have to lean forward to hear her. "I'm sorry. I never meant to hurt you or your boys."

I know how hard it must have been for her to apologize. I guess all I wanted was for her to acknowledge what she did, because the second she apologizes I feel all the tension leave my body. "Karen, we all make mistakes. Let's just move forward and like Valerie said, if you really are interested, we are happy to share what we know with you. You can call me anytime. Now let's put this behind us and move on."

I glance over at Sherry, who nods at me as Valerie and I get up. When we get outside, Valerie says, "Well, that went better than I anticipated."

"I know. I almost felt bad for her, but hopefully this will help. Now, what are you going to do about Lindsay's mom?"

"Nothing. I'm going to take the wait-and-see-what-happens approach. If Karen has any remorse, she will go back to Lindsay's mom and tell her she was wrong. If they are meant to go on a date it will work itself out. If not, there are plenty of fish in the sea and John will get over her. The part that upsets me is him thinking that she's rejecting him because of his diabetes. Unfortunately, there's not much I can do about that."

A few days later I get a text from Valerie. "Lindsay reached out to John and asked if they can reschedule their date. He is on cloud nine!"

I feel a wave of happiness and a sense of relief that I can now close the chapter on my relationship with Karen.

Fifty-seven

Over Thanksgiving, we fly north to visit my family, and when we arrive home, find our mailbox stuffed with two large envelopes! I grab the mail and run into the house, calling for Sean and David. Sean makes it to the living room first, but I convince him to wait for David and as soon he walks into the room, Sean tears into the first envelope. It's from Miami and I watch as his grin spreads from ear to ear. "I'm in!" he exclaims, as he looks over the letter and then passes it to David. The next envelope isn't hard to figure out. It has a big drawing of the Cocky mascot on it and again Sean's face lights up as he says, "And that's a YES from Carolina!" I'm fighting back the tears of joy as I watch him glow. Two down, one to go. We don't have to wait long. Three days later a big, orange envelope appears in our mailbox. Sean is at school, so I prop it up on the kitchen counter and call David.

"Well, a big orange envelope arrived today! Looks like we may have another yes!"

"Don't let him open it without me. I'll try to get home early."

As soon as I hear the door open, I dry my hands and greet Sean with a hug.

"How was your day?"

"It was good. I've got so much homework. Everyone is cramming in exams and papers before the holidays." He reaches into the refrigerator and grabs a snack. As he turns, he sees the envelope propped on the counter and looks over at me, nearly bursting with excitement.

"Dad will be home soon. Let's wait for him," I say, trying to contain my own excitement.

He nods and grabs his backpack. "Call me when he gets home. I'm going to start my work."

Finally, David walks through the door, and hearing his voice, Sean comes running into the kitchen. He grabs the envelope and tears it open.

"Three for three!" he yells, pumping his fist in the air.

I don't know why, but I'm so choked up I can barely speak. We share a group hug and Sean goes back to his homework while David goes to change. I'm so delighted for Sean that I decide to sit with that for a little while before I go into planning mode. Over dinner, we break-down the pros and cons for all three schools. The fact that Sydney was accepted to Clemson adds a big check mark to Sean's pro column. Abby had called earlier in the day to share the good news that Noah was accepted to all the schools he applied to, and according to Valerie, John is still waiting on one or two responses but did get into his first choice, which has shifted to NYU Tisch School of the Arts.

"Well, I guess this is really happening." I announce cheerfully, as I clear the plates from the table.

"Looks that way. Are you ready?" David asks. I lean into him, and he wraps his arms around me.

"I don't know if I'll ever be ready, but what I do know for sure is that I am so proud of him."

New Year's Eve, as has become our tradition, we host Abby and Frank along with Valerie and their boys. This year, Sydney, Brooke and Lindsay join us, adding to the festive atmosphere and I relish having a full house. The kids all spend the night with us and in the morning, we put out a spread of pancakes, waffles, eggs, bacon, and bagels. I quietly observe the kids as they sit around the table laughing, trying to shock each other with outrageous stories, and before they notice, I grab my camera and capture the moment.

Several weeks later, while we're eating dinner, Sean clears his throat.

"I've got an announcement. I've decided which college I want to attend."

David cups his hands around his mouth and in a deep, booming voice says, "Drum-roll, please."

I'm happy to oblige and begin to drum the table, which makes Sean wince and shake his head before declaring, "I've chosen University of Miami." He quickly looks from me to David, then back to me to gauge our reaction.

I jump up and hug him. "Sean, I am so excited for you! I think you'll love it there and are making a great choice."

"Mom, you can't say anything to Abby yet, but Noah chose Miami too! He's telling his parents tonight!"

"Sean, that's great news!" David says.

Silently, I say a prayer of thanks that there will be someone he can trust close by if he needs anything. David and I make a conscious effort to keep diabetes out of our decision-making when it comes to Sean's experiences, but the reality is that it's there and always will be. It won't be easy to be far away from him, but he is more than capable and extremely confident in how to care for himself. I know all this intellectually. Now, I just need to catch up emotionally.

The next morning, Abby calls as I'm leaving for the gym.

"Did Sean tell you the good news? He and Noah are going to college together!"

"I'm so thrilled, Abby. They are going to have the best time. How are you dealing with the distance?"

Abby hesitates before answering, "I'm ok. I'm trying to prepare myself, but I'm realizing it's going to be a huge adjustment when he leaves. I try not to think about it and just stay focused on getting him ready to go. I don't know why, but I never pictured him going that far. I really thought he'd end up at USC."

"Same here. For now, let's concentrate on finishing out the school year."

And that's exactly what I do. I work alongside the other parents on the senior committee to organize the senior assembly, adamant that I am going to live in the moment and soak it all up.

Fifty-eight

∞

I'm still sitting on the floor in the playroom, lost in my memories and mesmerized by the picture I'm holding of Sean wrapped in the fluffy blue towel, when David walks in and sits down next to me. His eyes move from mine to the photo I've now placed back in the album. I glance over at him and the words are out of my mouth before I can really process my thoughts.

"All these years later, I would give anything to go back to that one moment in time, that one moment where we were so ignorant to what was coming and I would embrace that little boy, so carefree, basking in the innocence of his childhood." As we flip through the pages that showcase the story of our family life — from the moment Sean was born to his first day of preschool, to the day he lost his first tooth — I lose myself in each photograph. My fingers trace over his sweet face as he lies sleeping in his first big boy bed, hugging Elmo. There he is sitting on the large dolphin at SeaWorld, and dancing with Mickey at Disney World. The basketball team photos, summer days building forts of sand on the beach, Halloweens as the Red Power Ranger and Buzz Lightyear. Each photo brings me back to the moment it was taken, and I am filled with love. I choose my favorites, which isn't easy because each picture holds a very special place in my heart. So many cherished memories.

Later that night Sean comes into our room before going to bed.

"Got a minute?" he asks.

"Of course." I pat the side of the bed and he sits down, looking serious.

"Noah and I have been talking about Miami and we've decided that we're going to apply for the same dorm, but we don't want to room together."

"Interesting," says David. "Care to elaborate on your reasoning?"

"We figure that if we have roommates, we will meet more people and have more of a college experience but still stay close by. We both want to make sure we branch out. Any thoughts?"

"I think that's a good decision," I say. "Will you set up a profile on the roommate selection site?"

"That's the plan. I just wanted to keep you in the loop."

He leans over and kisses my cheek, and I reach out to hug him. I seem to be holding on a little tighter and a little longer these days.

After he leaves David turns to me, shaking his head in wonder. "Our boy is really growing up!"

I nod and lean in for a hug before we turn off the light.

The day of the senior assembly all the kids wear T-shirts from the school they will be attending. A huge poster of the map of the United States hangs on the wall in the gymnasium. On a table below the poster is a box with pushpins. A balloon arch decorates the bleachers on the opposite side of the room, where they will take their class picture. In each corner of the room, enormous TV screens display a slide show of all the pictures the seniors submitted. I lean back against the wall and watch Sean with his group of friends. In my mind I see my little boy with his Thomas the Tank Engine backpack on his first day of pre-school. That sweet, innocent face has morphed into a young man before my eyes. I glance over and notice the principal greeting the students. Once they've all arrived, he officially welcomes them and congratulates them on their success. He runs through some statistics about the schools they will be attending and then, one by one, the kids walk over to the map and place their pins in the state where they will be attending college. I feel a lump in my throat as I watch Sean place his pin in the state of Florida. The photographer captures each student, and I capture Sean, then Noah and John. When the photographer gathers the class together for the group picture, I can't hold back anymore, and a few tears glide down my cheeks. I find a tissue and wipe them away, hoping nobody notices. I witness Sean, Noah and John standing together in the middle of the group with their arms around each other and I take some photos of my own, which I immediately text to Valerie, Abby and David. By the time we clean up and I walk to my car, I am exhausted, but my heart is full of gratitude for this school and these kids.

Graduation is beautiful. My heart bursts with joy when they call Sean's name, and we scream like little kids when he walks across the stage to shake Mr. Watson's hand and receive his diploma. Following the ceremony, everyone is running around taking pictures, tears are shed and promises to "stay in touch forever" are made. It's the end of a chapter in our lives that I have loved with all my heart.

Later that afternoon, Valerie and Abby come over to help me decorate for the graduation party we are hosting that evening. A few hours later, the house is full of laughter and chatter as our boys' friends, along with their parents, traipse in and out of the house. I'm amused, watching Sean in the family room, his arm around Sydney as they talk with a group of their friends. He looks up and we lock eyes, so I wink at him, and he playfully rolls his eyes before he turns his attention back to Sydney. He is beaming and I reach for my camera. I'm going to want to remember this moment.

Fifty-nine

We talk about splurging and taking a big trip, but in the end, we decide our annual trip to the beach would be the perfect way to celebrate graduation, and we are right. Five days of bliss for our family, and we love every moment of it. Once we are back home, there is so much to do. Sean has chosen a roommate, Jeff, who seems like a cool kid, and they have been texting to coordinate what they are each bringing. I look over the list and purchase the things Sean agreed to, along with his bedding and desk supplies, and a medical cooler to keep his insulin cold on the drive to Miami. I've dedicated one large bag solely to his diabetes supplies. As I load the bag with a three-month supply of each item he will need, I marvel at how far the technology has come. When he was first diagnosed, Sean had to stick his finger at least ten times a day to check his blood sugar. Now he wears his CGM and can open an app on his phone that tells him what his blood sugar reading is and how it is trending. Amazingly, this information transfers to an app on my phone, giving me piece of mind that if Sean suffers a low blood sugar in the middle of the night, the app will not only notify Sean, but I will receive an alert as well, offering me a little bit of comfort. As I finish packing his supplies, I say a little prayer that he will stay healthy and safe.

The night before we leave for Florida, we stop by Valerie's house to say good-bye to John. They are leaving in a few days to drive to New York City. The boys disappear as soon as we get there, so we sit on the porch with Valerie. David steps away to take a phone call as Valerie leans over and whispers in my ear.

"Are we really doing this? Are we really going to let them go to college?"

"Yes" I whisper back as I take her hand in mine. "We really are doing this."

"No one will ever understand what it will take to let them go."

I nod because I am too choked up to talk. As if on cue, Sean and John join us on the porch and we all hug. A few tears are shed as we say good-bye. John promises to keep in touch and we remind the boys of our plan to spend Thanksgiving together.

The next morning, David's car is literally bursting at the seams as we leave for Florida. The ride is long and tedious, but I hang on to every second. I'm in "organization" mode, so as soon as we get to the dorm, we follow the cones to the drop-off location and unload the car into big boxes on wheels. Once we unload, David goes to park the car, and I stay with our things while Sean goes to check in and get his keys. When he comes back, he is with another student who he introduces as Chuck. Together they start taking Sean's bags to his room while I wait for David. When he arrives, I give him the room number and he grabs some bags and the cooler of insulin and heads inside. It takes one more trip to get everything to the room, and then we all squeeze into the tiniest dorm room, where we meet Jeff and his parents. They seem like a fun family, and we chat amicably while we get the boys settled. I make Sean's bed while he hangs up his clothes, and David builds the hutch over Sean's desk. We are just about finished when the dorm resident advisor comes by to introduce himself, letting the boys know there is a floor meeting at five o'clock and then they will all eat dinner together.

It's four-thirty p.m. when David puts his hand on my back and quietly leans in to whisper, "It's time."

I glance up at him and instantly feel the stinging of tears forming in my eyes. Then I remember that it's impossible to cry if you smile, so I plaster a big smile on my face, tap Sean on the shoulder and ask, "Would you like to walk us down?"

He nods, and after we say goodbye to Jeff and his mom, who also looks like she is struggling, we take the elevator to the lobby. Once outside, I take Sean in my arms.

"I'm so proud of you. You are going to soar. Make good choices, work hard, and have a ton of fun. And remember I am only a phone call away. I love you."

"I will make good choices. I will work hard. And I plan on having a ton of fun!" He laughs, then hugs me a little tighter. "I love you too, Mom."

I kiss his cheek and move out of the way so David can say goodbye, and then David takes my hand, and we turn to go. I don't look back because I have lost all control, and I don't want him to see me cry.

An hour later my phone dings with a text message. "Heading to dinner with Jeff, Noah and some guys we met, then tonight going to the student center for some freshman activities. Will text you tomorrow. Love you guys."

I pause for a moment, my fingers hovering over the keyboard. What I want to write is

Remember to bring glucose tablets with you.

Pay attention to your CGM and watch your blood sugar.

Make sure the people around you know you have T1D.

I know in my heart it's time for him to fly, so with great restraint, I don't type any of those words. Instead, I send back a thumbs-up emoji and a silly "Have Fun" meme, and then I close my eyes and lean my head back against the seat, once again adjusting to my new normal.

A Message
from the Author

Thank you so much for reading my novel. While this story is a work of fiction, I did draw from my knowledge and personal experience raising a child with T1D. My goal in writing this book was to raise awareness about the challenges faced by those living with this disease. While this story centers around type 1 diabetes, it is my hope that parents will relate to these characters on multiple levels.

Breakthrough T1D (formerly JDRF) is a global organization and I am proud to say our family has been involved with them since our son was diagnosed. If you or someone you know has been diagnosed with type 1 diabetes, I strongly encourage you to learn more about them at www.breakthrought1d.org or reach out to your local Breakthrough T1D chapter. You don't have to do this alone.

The seeds for this story were planted during a conversation with my friend Lisa Lane. It was her encouragement and foresight that inspired me to write this story. Lisa introduced me to Julie Nye, an accomplished author, who mentored me through this process. If were not for Lisa and Julie, I'm not sure I would have had the courage to move forward with this novel. Special thanks to Marsha Zinberg, who took a very rough first draft and with honest feedback, direction and lots of red ink, helped me develop this story. A heartfelt thank you to my beta readers for taking the time to read my novel. Your feedback was invaluable.

I am blessed with a loving, supportive family and close friends who rallied around us, providing a soft spot to land when we were scared or overwhelmed in the earliest stages of our son's diagnosis. I am beyond grateful for our family and friends, most of whom were there from the beginning. Thank you for your support through the years — for walking with us, attending galas with us, donating on our behalf, lifting us up, and loving us through the years.

To my husband Brad, my love, my heart, my best friend. Your unwavering support through the years has meant so much to me. From the moment our son was diagnosed, we made a commitment to him that we would do everything in our power to help cure this disease. We are a formidable team, forever bonded, and together we have worked tirelessly to keep our promise.

Finally, to my son Justin. You are my reason. The pride I feel for you is immense. You live your life with such honor, dignity, grace and a sophisticated sense of humor. The only person who can make me laugh harder is your dad! Your ability to manage T1D and not let it define you is an inspiration. You are my hero and I love you with all my heart. Being your mom is the greatest honor of my life.

About the Author

Lori Schur is a retired event planner, a 'professional' volunteer, and now an author of her first novel "What Happened to Normal?" When her son was diagnosed with type 1 diabetes, Lori became involved with Breakthrough T1D, currently serving in a volunteer capacity as Chapter President of the Breakthrough T1D South Carolina Community Board of Directors and on the Breakthrough T1D Board Development Council. Through the years Lori has mentored newly diagnosed families, organized walk teams, and chaired several galas. She currently lives in Greenville, SC with her husband Brad.

Made in the USA
Columbia, SC
03 June 2025

58724701R00169